I0571100

MUST-HAVE HUSBAND

By
Ginny Baird

Published by
Winter Wedding Press

Edited by Linda Ingmanson
Cover by Dar Albert

About the Author

From the time that she could talk, romance author Ginny Baird was making up stories, much to the delight -- and consternation -- of her family and friends. By grade school, she'd turned that inclination into a talent, whereby her teacher allowed her to write and produce plays, rather than write boring book reports. Ginny continued writing throughout college, where she contributed articles to her literary campus weekly, then later pursued a career managing international projects with the US State Department.

Ginny's held an assortment of jobs, including school teacher, freelance fashion model, and greeting card writer, and has published more than ten works of fiction and optioned nine screenplays. She's additionally published short stories, nonfiction and poetry, and admits to being a true romantic at heart.

Ginny is the author of several bestselling romantic comedies, including novellas in her *Holiday Brides Series*. She's a member of Romance Writers of America (RWA), the RWA Published Authors Network (PAN), and the RWA Published Authors Special Interest Chapter (PASIC).

When she's not writing, Ginny enjoys cooking, biking and spending time with her family in Tidewater, Virginia. She loves hearing from her readers by email at GinnyBairdRomance@gmail.com and welcome visitors to her website at http://www.ginnybairdromance.com.

Chapter One

Connie Oliver bent forward to pick the brambles off her hiking socks. A manicured fingertip caught on the scratchy wool fabric and tore. She peered up through the bangs of her short blonde bob. "Excellent idea, sis. Totally awesome."

Linda gave an indignant pout. "Give me a break, will you? Just look. Look around! It's gorgeous."

Connie straightened in time to catch a fuzzy brown arachnid skittering up her leg. "Gorgeous, and full of spiders, ticks, and fleas!" she proclaimed, pulling it off with a pinch.

Linda watched her fling the bug into the forest then lifted an eyebrow. "Like those bloodsuckers back in Los Angeles are so much better."

"Now, don't you even go there. Just don't. You promised. No man talk, remember? This was supposed to be a girls' getaway."

"Yeah, yeah. I hear you. It's just that if you'd seen Walt for who he was in the first—"

"Linda!"

"Fine." She adjusted her baseball cap. "Deny it all you want. But you, girlfriend, have a talent for picking out losers."

"That's not true. I've just had bad luck."

"Bad luck since the eighth grade?"

"With a memory like yours, who needs iPhones?"

"Maybe we should have recorded it. Might have avoided instant replays."

Connie picked up her walking stick and moved along. "Like *you're* such an expert," she said, casting a scowl over her shoulder.

"I'm three years younger than you, and married, aren't I? To a great guy besides, because I know how to pick 'em." Linda hastened her pace to catch up, her long blonde ponytail bouncing. "Say... How about if Beau and I introduce you to—"

Connie hurried to stay ahead of her. "Another tomcat like Doctor Martin? No thank you."

Linda threw out her hands. "How were *we* supposed to know Beau's ethics professor was married with six children?"

"Ethics? Ha! So you see? I'm not the only one around here who makes mistakes."

"One mistake, okay?" She narrowed her thumb toward her forefinger. "One teeny little mistake..." She hustled to keep up. "Will you *puleeze* slow down?"

Connie halted in her tracks and met her sister's earnest blue gaze. "Beau's got a cousin..."

"No."

Linda's lips turned up in a grin. "Second cousin, twice-removed...?"

Connie huffed, feeling beaten down by this entire affair. Here she was, slated to get married in nine weeks, and she was absent one particular item: the groom. Not that it was entirely her fault. She'd had him at one point. He'd just unfortunately slipped away. "I said, no."

"Fine! Remain an old maid and break the family tradition. See if I care."

Connie took Linda by the elbow, stung by her barbs. "You know, Linda. If I didn't totally believe you love me... I'd swear you hate me."

Linda's expression softened. "Oh, Connie, I don't hate you, can't you see? I'm just worried about this predicament you've put yourself in."

Connie's mouth dropped open. "I didn't exactly ask Walt to walk out."

"No, hon, of course you didn't. But, can't you see? That was four *months* ago. And all this while plans for your wedding have been steamrolling along. You should have told them by now, Connie. Mom, Dad, Ollie... Everyone."

"Not *everyone*," she said, referring to their sickly older grandfather, "and you know it."

Linda warmly patted her shoulder. "If only I could help you face facts, then maybe you wouldn't keep doing this to yourself."

"Oh? And what facts are those?"

"You're a great girl from a wonderful family, but you can't seem to stop yourself from going after these tigers on the prowl."

Connie twisted her lips and stared at her sister. Inwardly, she knew that Linda was right. Connie *did* have a talent for picking out losers, but she'd never done it on purpose. Perhaps she was just too trusting, always wanting to see the good in everyone. "Just what are you saying?"

Linda stared at her sincerely. "Simply that you wouldn't know a decent man if he fell on you."

"Hey!"

"I mean it, Connie. There are tons of great people out there. Really good ones."

"Yeah, and as you keep reminding me, lots of bad ones too."

"I'm not encouraging you to keep going after the bad ones. All I'm saying is you need to be a little more flexible, not so rigid in your expectations."

"My expectations are the same as yours were," Connie lied. While she truly loved Beau and believed him perfect for Linda, the fact was his staid, mainstream conservatism didn't quite match her type. When Connie envisioned the ideal mate, he wasn't tall, coat-and-tie and conventional, but adventuresome, energetic, and fun. The problem with the energetic ones she'd had so far had been convincing them to focus all their energy on her. Connie sighed, wishing it weren't so darned difficult, this *happily ever after* thing.

"You know what Grandpa says…"

"*It's just as easy to love a rich man as a poor man,*" the two girls parroted together in a deep tone mimicking his, before bursting out in giggles.

Connie appraised her sister's carefree face, surmising it must feel wonderful to have met her special someone. Beau really was ideal for Linda and obviously made her happy. Connie felt a flash of envy, wondering if she'd ever know that sort of relationship herself. "Oh, Linda," she said, suddenly flinging herself into her sister's arms with a sob. "What am I going to do?"

Linda wrapped her arms around her and held her tight. "You're going to get through this, that's what. The moment we get back to Napa, you're going to tell everyone the truth."

Connie sucked in a breath, not knowing how she could possibly do that. The news would kill her grandfather, and he had one foot in the grave already. The only thing that kept him hanging on was the thought of living to see his last granddaughter wear the traditional family wedding gown, the one that had belonged to his late wife. With Connie, the cycle would be complete, and everyone destined to don the family heirloom and be blessed by its magic would have worn the sacred gown. Tears burned down her cheeks at the thought of breaking her dear grandfather's heart. He'd been so good to them all. It was a simple wish he'd held, not so unreasonable for a man of his generation.

She'd put off breaking the news to her family, hoping against hope the wedding might still go on. Perhaps Walt would come to his senses and realize she was the best thing that had ever happened to him. But just before Linda booked this girls' weekend, she'd learned that he'd already moved on. He'd not only taken up with someone new, he'd moved in with her besides. Connie released another sob, and Linda held her tighter.

"There, there," Linda said, patting her back. "It'll be okay."

Connie pulled back with a wail. "I don't see how!"

Perhaps Linda didn't either, because she had nothing further to offer. No kind words of wisdom or even snarky comments. She just studied her sister sadly.

"I feel so horrible I waited this long," Connie admitted, ashamed. "And now Grandpa's turning eighty."

"It might have been kinder to tell him *before* his birthday."

Connie blinked. "You're the one who was just saying now's the time to fess up!"

"And it is," Linda said surely. "The longer you let this go on, the worse for everyone it's going to be. You're going to have to just woman up and put it out there. It will be like a Band-Aid, ripping it off."

"Ow!"

"But the sooner it's done…" Linda held her gaze. "The sooner everyone will begin to heal. You included, sister. You've got to take this next step, so your life can go forward."

Rugged mountain man "Mac" McCormack strode through the main room of the rustic lodge, carting his gear. The rucksack strapped to his shoulders carried a pup tent, bedroll, sleeping bag, and all the dehydrated foods an outdoorsman could hope for.

His best friend, Hank, and the owner of the lodge, addressed him from the far side of the reception desk. "Headed out already? I thought you weren't breaking camp until dawn?"

Mac stopped and turned toward his friend, stroking his reddish beard. It had come in nice and full and slightly darker than the auburn hair on his head. It matched his fur elsewhere, though. "I feel a rain coming on," he told Hank. "So I wanted to stake out early."

"Speaking of getting soaked…" Hank leaned forward, resting his elbows on the desk. "What did the insurance dudes say about your store?"

Mac shifted on his feet, disgruntled by the memory. "Just what I expected. There's an out clause in my coverage excluding forest fires.

"Ouch, man. That burns. What are you going to do?"

"What I always do when the going gets tough. Hit the trail."

Hank lowered dark eyebrows over chocolate-colored eyes. "If you're coming back by Saturday, maybe you could double up with Kelly and me? We're grabbing a burger, then a movie in town. I'm betting we could talk her sister Victoria into coming along."

"No, thanks."

"No? Just like that?"

"Let me guess. She's a brunette and beautiful, with a teeny little…" He gripped his bottom, then cupped his hands in front of his chest. "And great big…"

Hank stared at him in disbelief. "You've got a problem with that?"

"I've got a problem with all your setups, Hank."

"Why?"

"Because the girls you pick out for me are the ones you want for yourself." He walked away, whistling brightly.

"Hey!" Hank called after him. "She's a redhead! Scottish background just like you!"

"Not interested," Mac continued in a singsongy voice, making his way toward the door.

"You're going to wind up a bachelor if it kills you."

Mac stopped walking and turned slowly on his heels. "I'm not going out on a limb for just any woman," he said, meeting his friend's gaze. "She's got to be special. You know, *have it*."

"What's *it*?" Hank asked with dismay. "You aching to hear angels sing or something?"

Mac considered this. "Maybe." He removed his pack, set it down, and pulled a rain poncho from a forward zipper. Hank glanced out the broad picture window framing the mountains and valley.

"What makes you so sure it's going to rain? Sky's as clear as a bell."

Mac slipped on his poncho. "Any man's been hiking these hills as long as I have tends to develop a sense of things. Foreknowledge, some might say. Others call it intuition." He shifted the pack back onto his shoulders and a satellite phone slid from his jeans pocket, smacking against the redwood floor.

"Foreknowledge?" Hank loudly cleared his throat. "Looks more like weather.com to me."

Rain beat down harder as Connie and Linda cowered beneath the canopy of an incense cedar. Connie steadied the soggy trail map in her hands but couldn't make heads or tails of it in the drowning rain. "I think we go… No, wait a minute."

"Might help if you turned it right-side up. Here, let me see that." Linda snatched away the map, and it tore in a jagged line down the middle.

"Great, Linda! Really super." Connie shook out her dripping half of the page. "Look what you've done now."

Lightning split the sky, and the girls huddled closer together.

"Sorry," Linda said with a grimace.

"Try your cell again," Connie urged.

Linda took it from her jacket pocket, sheltering its face with her hand.

"Still nothing doing?"

Linda's eyes registered worry. "Not a bar."

Thunder boomed as darkness shrouded the forest, settling between towering redwoods and ponderosa pines.

"Night's falling."

Linda swallowed hard, panning the dense landscape. In their effort to take shelter from the storm, they'd wandered off the trail. Now that everything was covered in a deep sludge, they couldn't find it at all. "Uh-huh."

"Don't panic." Connie wrapped an arm around her little sister. "This is one of those summer things. It will blow over."

"Sure, and then what?"

"Then… Well, I don't know! We'll think of something. It's not like we'll be stuck out here forever."

Linda's chin trembled as she shook her head. Connie met her sister's panicked gaze, knowing just what she was thinking. They *were* going to be stuck out here forever. Eventually, nothing would be found of them…except for a few scattered bones that had been picked over by grizzly bears.

"Linda?" Connie asked, her voice warbling.

Linda's voice trembled in return. "Huh?"

"Oh my Gawd!" they shouted in unison, gripping one another.

Mac shimmied up a spreading oak, his hiking boots slipping on the damp trunk. The rain had stopped an hour ago, leaving everything in the forest soaked. He steadied himself and climbed higher, his food bag on a rope and pulley secured around his waist. He wouldn't have any bears stealing his grub this time. He damn well couldn't afford it. Not with his business, as well as his dreams of financial security, having gone up in smoke. His feet slid again, and he paused, glancing down below. He'd been lucky to get his tent pitched before the downpour. Thankfully, he'd been able to keep everything dry, including some wood and kindling sticks he'd collected and covered over with a tarp. Wasn't easy to build a campfire when the logs were as soaked as this towering tree. Mac gritted his teeth and clambered up another few feet. He spotted the perfect branch overhead. Once he had this in place, he'd head back down and cozy up by the fire. Even in summertime, the nights here got pretty chilly. But Mac knew how to handle that. He was good with the outdoors and never missed a beat. Yessirree. He was a fellow who always knew just what he was doing.

Connie forged ahead as Linda clung to her arm. "Remind me to kill you if we live through this."

"Oh, we'll live, all right. Then you're going to be the one who needs protection—from our entire family."

"Thanks."

Linda stumbled, but Connie shored her up. "We'll need to watch our step."

"No kidding. Thank goodness that was just a stick and not a snake."

"Snake?" Connie stared at her in panic. If there was one thing Connie couldn't stand, it was anything that slithered. Fact was, she didn't care much for creepy-crawlies either. *A weekend in the wild. How in the world did I let Linda talk me into this?*

"You blame me, don't you?" Linda asked.

"I didn't say that."

"No, but you were getting all mysteriously quiet, like you do when you think I've come up with a bad idea."

"I'm sure it wasn't your idea for us to get lost."

"No, but—"

Connie held up her hand, scanning the woods ahead. She thought she spied a glimmer of light beyond a stand of pines. "Linda, look!"

"Where?"

"Over there. I think I see something."

Linda shivered, seizing her by the elbow. "You mean like something big, with long, sharp teeth?"

"Stop being such a chicken," Connie scolded. Night noises sounded all around them, and Connie gripped her sister's hand.

"Now who's being the baby?" Linda whispered.

"Shh!" She pulled Linda forward. "Come on, I think it's a campfire."

"Are you sure we should go through that thicket? Could be loaded with scary things."

"There'll be less of those around the fire," she said, giving Linda's hand a tug. "Let's go."

As they made their way through the thick brush, Connie saw she'd been right. It was a campfire for sure. Neatly ringed by large stones and blazing in its glory. There was a tent set up nearby. A tin coffeepot sat on a flat rock by the fire, beside a single mug.

"Where are the campers?" Linda asked under her breath.

Connie whispered, her voice trembling. "Maybe the bears got them."

"Very funny."

"I wasn't trying to be."

Just then, the two heard rustling overhead. The girls looked up with a start, spotting a dark figure shimmying down the tree and moving toward them.

This was it. Connie knew it. She and her baby sister were about to become something's dinner. How she wanted to run. Bolt like a streak of light straight to that fire and beyond. Pick up a club, weapon, coffeepot... Huh? Well, anything! Maybe one of those very big stones over there. Yeah, that would work. If only she could get her feet to move. But they were stuck like lead in quicksand.

"Connie!" Linda said softly. "Let's go!" She yanked on Connie's arm. But Connie just stood there, mesmerized, transfixed by the fact that she was living out her final moments. Destiny had a way of catching up with everybody, so maybe it was time she met her fate. She'd deceived her family into thinking she was still getting married, letting them go to a lot of unnecessary trouble and expense. And now she was going, to pay…in spades. Maybe if the beast filled up on her, he'd be too full to gobble up her sister. "*Connie!*" Linda wrapped two hands around Connie's wrist and tugged with all her might, yanking her up and off her feet.

"Ahh!" Connie screeched as something loud bellowed from above.

A split second later, heaven and earth came crashing down in a heap, landing in a huge mass in the very spot where Connie had just stood. She stared at Linda agape. "You saved my life!"

"Yeah, but from what?"

They stared down at the pile of branches and leaves shielding a groaning form. "Oohhh. Aahh."

Linda cupped her mouth with a hand.

"What is it?" Connie asked.

"A bear?" Linda offered uncertainly.

"Since when do bears make those kinds of noises?"

"I don't know. I don't speak bear."

Connie squinted through the darkness as rays of light from the campfire cast a sporadic glow on their subject. She cautiously inched forward and gingerly lifted a branch.

"Don't get too close," Linda warned.

Connie stared in disbelief at two slightly worn hiking boots protruding from under the mass. "Oh my goodness."

"I knew it! It's a bear!"

Connie lifted another branch, then sucked in a breath. "It's a *man*."

"A *what*? What was he doing up there?"

As if in answer, a long coil of rope spiraled down from the trees, dropping in a heap on top of the leafy pile. Linda reached forward and picked up the rope, which dangled in something like a hangman's noose.

"Oh my God," Connie gasped.

"Yeah. Totally."

Mac thought he'd heard talking beneath him, but that was unlikely in this part of the woods. Maybe he'd had such a long day he was hearing things. He had the rope almost set, but decided to prop it in the crook of a branch and leave it a sec to check out the noises below. Maybe some wildlife was searching for kibbles around the fire. He'd need to scoot down and shoo it away before finishing his work.

He was halfway down the tree when his darned boots slipped again, causing him to skid. Maybe if he grabbed that branch over there to steady himself, he'd be able to ease down slowly. But no! The branch snapped unexpectedly, hurtling him into the darkness below.

The next thing Mac knew, his back ached and his head was killing him. To make matters worse, there appeared to be whispering around him, as prickly prongs poked at him from every which way. *Is it my imagination, or did something just kick my boot?*

This is one hell of a hangover, he thought before passing out again.

Chapter Two

"Don't kick him!" Connie yelped.

"I'm just trying to see if he's, um…with us."

"Alive, you mean? Good God, Linda. Let's unbury him."

"Bad choice of words."

"Sorry."

They got to work quickly, casting aside the branches and leaves.

"Wow, he's a man all right," Linda said as firelight from the campfire illuminated his handsome face. "A darned good-looking one at that."

"Linda! Now's not the time to think about good-looking!" Although she had to admit her sister had a point. He was pretty hot. Even in that position.

"Come on," Linda said, "help me get him over to the fire so we can examine his wounds."

"You don't move a man who's fallen."

"You're right."

Connie set her chin in one hand while resting her elbow in the other. "Maybe we should try talking to him? Getting him to come around?"

A soft voice carried on the night wind, calling Mac out of his slumber. "Um, sir? Are you all right?" He awakened to find lovely blue eyes peering into his own. They were set in the face of an angel with short blonde hair and lovely pale skin. She radiated heaven's glow, a soft ring of light from beyond framing her head.

"You're an angel?" he asked, scarcely able to believe it. He thanked the heavens for sending one approximately his age. That was what they called divine providence. Or so he thought. He couldn't remember that far back in church school, not that he'd be mentioning this to St. Peter.

She pursed her lips a beat and stared at him. "Um, no. Not really."

He got it. She was one of those messenger types. An angel wannabe, waiting to earn her wings. And, boy, how he wanted to help her, do any little thing she wanted… If only his head didn't smart so much. He tried lifting it, then set it back down with a thunk, grimacing at the pain.

"Do you think you can move?" she asked in a voice so sweet Mac thought he heard a chorus of harp strings.

"I'm not sure," he answered hoarsely.

"Ask him if anything's broken," another voice said from nearby.

Mac rolled his eyes toward the clearing, spying another angel, a bit smaller than this one… Wait a minute. Wearing a Los Angeles Dodgers baseball cap? Mac sat up with a start, and little birds began chirping all around him, darting through flecks of light. "I think I need to lie back down."

As his eyelids fluttered shut, Mac thought he spied flames lapping the darkness in the distance. He hoped that wasn't a bad sign. He didn't seem to be thinking too straight at the moment. *The Dodgers. Well, I'll be. I never knew God played favorites.*

Connie stared at her sister as the man passed out again. Thunder rumbled above and little flecks of rain began to strike the surrounding foliage.

"Oh no. Not again."

"What are we going to do?" Connie asked with despair.

Linda adjusted her cap against the rain that was streaming down harder. "We need to get him to shelter."

Connie agreed. Though she couldn't see for the life of her how she and her petite little sister were going to move this bear of a man. "I know, but we certainly can't carry him."

Linda shook her head. "How about if we drag him?"

"By what? His beard?"

"Hang on. Keep him dry."

Linda scurried away toward the tent as Connie angled herself over the guy, holding her jacket out sideways to keep as much moisture off as possible. "Hurry it up, will ya?" she called back to Linda, who seemed to be taking her time in the tent.

"Got it!" her sister proclaimed, emerging with a curled-up bedroll.

A makeshift stretcher. What a great idea! "You're a genius," she told Linda as her sister carted the piece over and unrolled it next to the man.

"Okay, now help me," Linda instructed. "Let's get the top end first."

Connie bent low to grip the guy under one arm, while Linda grabbed him by the other.

"On three! Watch his head, now. *One... Two...*"

Goodness, he weighed a ton.

"*Three!*"

"*Harrumph.*" Both girls tugged together, sliding the top part of the man's torso onto the bedroll. The rain drove down harder, flecking his flannel shirt and dampening their clothes.

"Better hurry it up," Connie urged.

They got his legs on next, then prepared to tug from the head end of the bedroll. "Are you sure this will work?" Connie asked. "What if we injure him further?"

"What if he drowns in the rain?"

"You're right."

Seconds later, they gave the bedroll a tug. Nothing happened. They met each other's gazes, then yanked harder. The man's hands and arms flopped to the side. "Oh no!"

Then one of his feet spilled off the bedroll too.

"We've got to keep him in place somehow," Connie called through the rain that by now was drenching their clothing.

Linda adjusted her cap and scanned the area. Quickly, she took up the rope that had fallen out of the trees.

"You want us to rope him?" Connie asked in shock.

"Just temporarily."

Connie watched Linda take charge employing some sort of skill she'd supposedly learned in Girl Scouting. Although Linda's time in the Scouts had been limited to one year in the second grade, and Connie didn't believe Brownies were primed in tying people up.

"Why don't you just pop an apple in his mouth and be done with it?"

"Stop it." She finished her work, securing his wrists and ankles together, and somehow linking both ends before tying him to the bedroll. Linda turned expectant eyes on her sister. "Well? Are you going to help me, or aren't you?"

"Yeah, sure." Connie bent toward the man, hoping to goodness he wouldn't remember this. This was the kinkiest thing she'd ever done. Even if it was for the right reasons. As she positioned herself near the top of the bedroll, Connie raised an eyebrow at her sister. "Where did you *really* learn that thing with the ropes? Did Beau teach you?"

"You, sister, have an all-too-vivid imagination," she said as they heaved the bedroll forward.

Connie and Linda sat beside the prone man in the cramped space of the tent while rain pitter-pattered above. He just lay there snoozing, looking none too worse for the wear, considering the beating he'd taken. He stood about six feet tall and was fairly broad at the shoulders, well built with a solid chest. He was obviously athletic and kept himself in shape, most likely by doing rugged outdoor stuff like mountain climbing. Although considering he couldn't even climb a tree without falling, maybe scaling mountains wasn't such a good idea.

Connie glanced at her sister, who was neatly coiling the rope. They'd found a battery-powered lantern with his gear, and it now illuminated the small area. "What are we going to do with him?"

"Get him to help, if we can."

"How can we help him when we don't even know where we are?"

"Good point."

Connie studied his chiseled face in the lantern's glow, wondering how he'd look without the beard. Not that it didn't suit him. It most certainly did, giving him the air of a man of the wild. Someone who was confident—and comfortable—with nature. She fought an urge to reach out and stroke his cheek, just to see how it felt. She'd never dated anyone with facial hair.

"Connie," Linda cautioned. "What are you doing?"

She looked down with a start to see she'd very nearly touched him. "I, uh…" She drew her fist to her mouth, faking a cough. "Was just warming my fingers by the lantern."

Linda gave her a suspicious look. "Sure you were." She surveyed his face, addressing her sister. "He *is* pretty cute. You've got to admit it."

"Yes. If only he weren't"—Connie lowered her voice—"suicidal."

"So maybe he was down on his luck?"

"That's a pretty drastic way out. And you know it."

A devious smile spread across Linda's lips. "I wonder if he'd consider coming to Napa?"

"*What?*"

"I mean, just for a rest. You know, to recoup from his"—she eyed the coil of rope nearby—"dreadful ordeal."

"Are you out of your mind? We can't take a strange man back to Napa."

"He'd couldn't be any stranger than Walt. Or…? What was the name of the guy before?

"Jake."

"That one was a nutcase. Whoohoo. Real Looney Tunes."

Connie heaved a breath. "We don't even know who this guy is."

"Maybe we should check his pants? Look for ID?"

Both girls eagerly sprang forward.

"I'll check," Linda said, kneeling beside him and angling her hand over his jeans.

"You're married!" Connie elbowed in. "Let me do it."

Linda lifted an eyebrow and sat back on her haunches. "Well, go on. Don't be shy about it," she said as Connie wiggled her fingers into the man's right front pocket. "Go for the gold."

"Stop it. I think I just found a"—she extracted a thin leather billfold—"wallet."

Linda snatched it away.

"Hey!"

Before she could stop her, Linda was scanning through a row of credit cards. "Aha!" she said, withdrawing a driver's license. "We have before us one Adam McCormack, but apparently," she said, flipping through an assortment of billfold photos, "he goes by Mac."

"How do you know that?"

"It's who all these women have autographed their photos to."

Connie twisted her lips, thinking it was no wonder. When this guy was in his right mind, he was probably quite a catch.

"Well, well…" Linda baited. "Will you look at *her*. And what a cutie too. I'll bet this one was his favorite," she said, thumping her finger against one picture in particular.

Connie raised her brow, and Linda turned the billfold in her direction. The worn color photo was of the most adorable yellow lab and a little boy, roughly ten years old. "Aw. Do you think that's him? I mean, Mac? As a kid?"

"I'm guessing, yeah." Linda closed the wallet and handed it to Connie. "Kind of sentimental. Keeping a photo of his first dog. Don't you think?"

Connie's heart softened, thinking this man couldn't be all bad. Life must have been awfully hard on him to push him so far over the edge.

Mac's eyelids fluttered, and she shoved the wallet back in his pocket. He reached up and grabbed her wrist before she could withdraw her hand.

"Well, hey," he said groggily.

Connie felt her face flame "Um. Hello," she offered weakly. "I was just checking your...credentials."

"That makes sense." He smiled warmly. "Wouldn't want to tag the wrong body."

She felt herself flush brighter. "No."

She tried to pull her arm away, but he held her fast with a quizzical look. "Am I dead yet?"

"Of course no—"

"Yes!" Linda yelped with enthusiasm.

Mac raised his head to peer at her.

Connie set her jaw and glanced at Linda before shooting Mac an apologetic look. "Will you excuse us one second?"

She motioned her sister to the far side of the tent, then hissed in a whisper, "Just what do you think you're doing?"

"What? Dead could work." Her cheeks took on a rosy glow. "We could tell him Napa is heaven."

Connie gasped. "I can't believe you said that."

"It's just a little lie."

"You really have flipped your lid."

"Think about it, Connie. He could come home with us, be there for Grandpa's birthday."

"As what?"

"Your betrothed, of course. That way, you wouldn't have to ruin the party with your news. We could play this little game to get you through it, then—"

"Absolutely not. You're talking crazy."

"We could get him help," her sister tempted. "Secure the best psychiatric care money can buy."

She fumed at Linda's ludicrous suggestion. "And here stands the woman, who—not hours ago—was telling me that now's the time to fess up. Come clean with the whole family."

She pinned Linda in place with her stare. After a prolonged beat, Linda dropped her eyes, awash with shame. "You're right. It was a stupid idea. I never should have mentioned it."

Mac shook his head, trying to clear it. It still hurt quite a bit and his body ached all over, but he was built tough and would soon get over it. He'd had the wind knocked out of him before and had always recovered. What he didn't get was why his wrists felt raw. He massaged them, studying them curiously. *Wait a minute. Is that rope burn?*

Mac raised his brow at the women whispering on the far side of the tent. They both turned to look at him. "You're sitting up!" the one in the baseball cap said.

But it was the other girl with the short blonde hair who held his attention. He chuckled to himself, thinking he'd envisioned her as an angel when he was still coming to. Of course, that halo must have been the campfire's glow illuminating her from behind. And then when he'd nearly caught her feeling him up, it was all he could do to keep a straight face. Going for his credentials, right. She'd blushed so brightly when he caught her with her hand down his pants, he couldn't help making that joke about being dead. For some weird reason, though, the girls didn't seem to find it funny at all. In fact, he had the notion they'd taken him seriously.

When the women scooted toward him, Mac decided maybe he should have taken himself seriously too. For when he looked in his angel's eyes, it was like he'd died and gone to heaven. They were pale blue like the sky on a springtime day, and her lips were full and kissable. Man, she was a knockout with those nice long legs and that lean athletic body. He wondered briefly if she was as outdoorsy as he was. Then she drew closer and he caught a whiff of her perfume, deciding *nope*. No wilderness girl went out in nature sweetening themselves up for insects that way.

"How are you feeling?" she asked, lifting her brow in concern. The other woman's face also looked worried.

"Better. But I don't think I should stand yet. Best to give it a little time."

"Uh-huh," both girls agreed.

The shorter one adjusted her baseball cap, and Mac noted she was wearing a wedding band set next to an enormous rock of an engagement ring. His gaze casually panned down his angel's arm to her delicately manicured fingertips, noting one of her nails had broken. Definitely not a nature girl, *and definitely not married*, Mac mused to himself, thinking he'd picked just right. Mac drew a breath, scarcely believing himself. What was he doing, thinking of choosing and looking for wedding bands? He must have taken a much harder knock to his noggin than he'd imagined. He coughed and pointed to his water across the way.

"Do you think you could hand me that canteen over there?"

The smaller girl reached for it while the other one just sat there, staring in his eyes. Mac wondered if she'd noticed him checking for a ring and felt his face warm beneath his beard. He had to get a grip. He didn't even know her name.

"My name's Connie," she said, smiling sweetly. "I'm the one you nearly fell on back there."

"Fell on? I'm so sor—"

"And *I'm* the one who saved her," the other one proclaimed, butting in as she passed him the canteen. "I'm Linda."

"Nice to meet you both. I'm Mac."

"We know," they parroted together.

Mac raised an eyebrow. "Are you two twins or something?"

"Sisters," Connie said.

"She's older," Linda added.

"I see." He studied them both, attempting to devote equal attention to each, but it was tough to pull his gaze away from pretty Connie. "Just what were you girls doing out here anyway? It's not really safe to be wandering around at night."

"Don't we know it!" Linda said.

"We went hiking." Connie shrugged. "But we got lost."

Linda explained further. "We ran for shelter during the storm and got off the trail."

"Never a good thing to do," he told them. "Stray off the trail, particularly when you're not used to being outdoors."

Connie set her hand on her hip and flipped her hair to the side. "What makes you think we're not used to being outdoors?"

He glanced at her chipped fingernail, then once more met her eyes. "Wild guess."

"Huh!" she said, acting slightly indignant.

"He's right, Connie," Linda said. She turned her gaze on Mac's. "The truth is we've never gone hiking before. It was kind of my idea, a girls' getaway to help Connie forget—"

Connie reached out a hand to cover her sister's blabbermouth. What *was* it about Linda sometimes? The girl couldn't keep herself from talking! Connie didn't know why she particularly cared if Mac knew she'd come up here on the run from heartache, but she did. Besides, it wasn't her sister's business sharing the news. "She means we came up here to escape the city. Forget about those everyday pressures. Unwind in the fresh air, you know? Only we didn't expect the air to turn windy or rainy…or for it to get dark. Um. Yeah. That."

Mac studied her in a curious way, and she dropped her hand away from Linda's pursed lips. There was an awkward beat during which Connie felt her skin warm from her head down to her toes. His eyes were hazel, a heady mixture of green and brown, changing subtly in the dim light. He was one fine specimen of a man, if she'd ever seen one. A real he-man, with that well-trimmed beard and mustache that made him look like a Scottish lord or highland mountaineer. Connie envisioned him wearing a kilt and sweeping her into his arms. He was clearly strong enough to do it.

He gave her a tilted smile, and her pulse fluttered. "In that case, it's a good thing we all ran into each other."

"Uh-huh," Connie answered weakly.

Linda elbowed her, then whispered in her ear, "What's wrong with you? You look faint."

"I'm fine, just fine," she spouted back in low tones.

"I mean," he continued, "I didn't drop breadcrumbs, but I certainly know the way home."

"That's great!" Linda said.

"Should we head back tonight?" Connie asked.

"Now, even *I'm* too smart to do that," Mac said with a wink. He glanced heavenward as the tiny pings of rain began to fade. "Sounds like it's letting up out there. Once the rain passes, I'll go and stoke that fire again. I'll bet you two are pretty hungry."

Connie's stomach rumbled in spite of herself. "Just a little." The truth was she was ravenous. Neither she nor Linda had eaten since morning.

"A little? I'm starved!" Linda looked eagerly at Mac. "Got any steaks in your pack?"

"How about some gruel and hardtack?" He laughed out loud at their stunned expressions. "You girls don't go camping much, do you?"

"I think we were wrong about him," Connie whispered to Linda.

"What do you mean?"

They were in the tent where Mac had insisted they bed down while he took the bedroll next to the fire. He'd prepared them a delicious dinner from dehydrated veggies and pasta that had tasted as good to Connie as a meal at Fellini's. It was just a shame they hadn't had a nice Chianti to go with it. Connie could have used a glass or two. But the truth was she didn't really need any alcohol. She was so exhausted from the day she'd likely sleep like a log.

"About that…" She made a gagging motion around her throat. "You know."

"I wouldn't be so sure, Connie. He still could be troubled."

"He seems fine to me."

"So, maybe we brightened his day?"

They lay face-to-face under Mac's warm sleeping bag, while he roughed it in his layered clothing outdoors.

"Do you think he's all right out there?" Connie asked.

"He's used to it."

"Well, I'm not." She struggled to get comfortable atop the rock-hard ground. "This certainly isn't the Ritz."

"Don't be such a spoily, and be glad we found him. Or he found us."

"Nearly killed us."

"You in particular."

"Dropped right out of the sky."

The girls giggled.

"He *is* pretty hot, Connie. You can't say you didn't notice the color of his eyes."

"They were…unusual."

"He's dishy. If I weren't so happily married, I'd make a meal of him my—"

Connie swatted her arm. "Shut up!"

They giggled again like two kids at a campout.

"It's not too late to ask him…"

"We are *not* inviting him to Napa," Connie said firmly. "Okay?"

Linda shrugged, turning away. "Suit yourself."

After a prolonged moment, Connie tapped Linda on the shoulder and whispered, "What do you think it's like?"

"What?"

"Kissing a man with a beard?"

"I wouldn't know." She turned back toward her sister with a devilish grin. "But something tells me you'd like to."

Connie shook her head and settled back down. "Let's get some sleep."

Within minutes, she heard Linda snoring softly. She'd done it since she was a baby and had never outgrown it. Poor Beau was a saint to put up with that.

Connie rolled onto her side, watching the flames from the campfire cast shadows across the tent wall. She didn't see any other movement and couldn't hear anything, so she decided that Mac must be sleeping as well. And that was a good thing too, because at that precise moment Connie felt nature call. She kicked herself for not going when Linda went earlier, but she hadn't had the urge. Now that she did, her sister was out cold. After such a long day, it would be unfair to wake her, and she certainly wasn't going to trouble Mac to be her escort on a potty run. She flushed with embarrassment at the thought.

Connie crept from the tent and slipped around behind it, going in the opposite direction of the fire. She didn't dare go too deep in the woods. Goodness knew, she could get lost again. Still, she couldn't stay too close. What if Mac were to awaken and see her? She'd positively die. Connie glanced over her shoulder, thinking that as long as she kept the light from the campfire in view, she'd be able to make her way back just fine.

Suddenly, she heard a twig snap. Connie froze in her tracks, her heart beating faster. Leaves rustled nearby and she felt a rush of panic. What if it was a bear? A snake? A coyote? *Or worse?* She wasn't sure what could be worse than any of those, unless it was the three of them together. Connie swallowed hard, her eyes darting back toward the camp. Maybe she should make a break for it, run like crazy toward the fire. And wake up Mac? Over something probably silly, like a little forest creature?

The rustling noises grew louder as a dark shadow loomed near. Wait! It was turning. Moving in her direction! *Run,* she told her legs, but they stayed in place, like two posts cemented in the earth. *Move, move, come on.*

"I'm going to die!" Connie wailed as it broke through the trees.

"Connie?" Mac raised his flashlight and pointed it in her direction.

"Mac!" she cried with relief, leaping at him. He dropped the wood he'd gathered in his arms to catch her. "Hang on there. What's going on?"

"I thought you were a bear!"

"Are you hinting that I should shave?" he teased lightly.

"What?" she asked, looking up at him. She was positively pale, on the verge of collapse.

"What were you doing in the woods?"

"I had to…um. Nature was calling."

"Is it still?"

"Huh?" she asked weakly.

"Did you go, Connie? Relieve yourself, I mean."

She shook her head, her chin trembling.

"Okay, then. Why don't you go on about your business?"

"Here?"

"Yes, here." He chuckled and straightened her, patting her firmly on the shoulders. "I'll be over there"—he nodded toward the edge of the clearing—"standing guard."

He handed her the flashlight. "Why don't you keep this. It might help."

Mac gathered up the wood he'd dropped and left Connie to her privacy.

"You won't go far?" she asked, her voice rising.

"Just holler if you need me."

A few minutes later, Connie hurried back through the trees and scurried past Mac, passing off the flashlight. "Thanks again," she said quickly, shielding her face with her hand to hide her embarrassment. Her skin felt as hot as those campfire flames right now.

"Any time!" he called after her as she dashed back in the tent.

"Where were you?" Linda asked, sitting up.

Connie sat down beside her, folding her face in her hands.

"Don't even ask."

Chapter Three

Mac steeled himself against the pain in his ankle as they made their way downhill. He figured he must have landed on it wrong when falling out of that blasted tree. He'd wrapped it last night with the bandage he kept in his first aid kit, hoping that the added support would help. It had worked just fine until he'd started really moving this morning, breaking down his campsite and leading these two city girls down the mountain. Mac was glad they'd happened across his campsite. He didn't know what might have become of the two of them in the wilderness if they hadn't had that luck.

He spotted the lodge just up ahead. They were almost home free. Hank worked part-time as an EMT, so he could take a look at Mac's ankle, and the girls would be returned to the safety of society. Well, about as much of it as one could find in these parts anyway. He held back the huge wooden door to the lodge, allowing Connie and Linda to enter ahead of him.

"You're limping," Connie said, her pretty mouth creased with worry lines.

"We need to get him seen," Linda added, barreling ahead. She beelined for the reception desk, where Hank awaited her with an expectant expression.

"Can I help you?" he asked, recognizing her as one of the two ladies staying in Room 214.

She shot him a concerned look. "Is there a doctor in the house?"

Hank cast a curious glance at his gimpy friend. "I'm certified in first aid."

She leaned forward with a confidential whisper. "I mean a *head doctor*. You know, a psychiatrist? Psychologist. Whatever."

Hank blinked, wondering just what had gone on between Mac and these two. "You just happen to be in luck," he returned in low tones. "I'm in therapy."

"Oh!" she said, not understanding. "What kind?"

"What kind do you need?"

She lowered her voice even further. "That man over there…"

"Mac?"

She nodded, meeting his gaze. "He tried to hang himself."

Hank knew Mac had been feeling down, but didn't think things had gotten that bad. "Seriously?"

"I think you'd better have a look at his ankle," the taller girl said, assisting Mac by the elbow as they ambled forward.

"Yes," Hank agreed, meeting Mac's eyes. "It seems we need to tal—" He stopped himself, putting on his best doctor voice. "What I mean is… Indeed, a full examination is in order." He grabbed a clipboard and a pair of glasses from the check-in desk. "If you ladies will excuse us."

Hank shut the door to his office behind them as Mac stumbled against him. "Good God," he quipped with surprise. "You can still stand, can't you?"

Mac hobbled over and took a seat in a nearby chair. "I'm fine."

"How's the recall?"

"Excellent, why?"

Hank walked over and thumped him on the chest. "Because, buddy boy. I'm going to want every lurid detail. Starting from how you twisted that ankle to what you were doing in the woods with two hot—" He stared at Mac's wrists, then met his eyes. Whoa, buddy. He had no clue Mac was into that stuff. "Are those rope burns?"

"I have no idea how those got there. Maybe when I fell out of that tree, my wrists caught on something."

"Likely story."

"What?"

"Keep your little secrets for all I care. Sometimes you think you know a man…"

"Listen, Hank. There was nothing kinky going on, if that's what you're getting at. I was just up in a tree with my rope when—"

Hank gasped with surprise. "Were you up there trying to kill yourself?"

"What? No!"

"Then what gave those girls the idea you were?"

Mac's eyes panned toward the office door. "I have no idea."

"Well, they're both really concerned about you." He slowly stroked his chin. "You sure hit pay dirt with this one."

"What on earth are you talking about?"

"That pot of gold at the end of the rainbow. Get it? The yellow brick road!"

"Huh?"

Hank blinked. "Wait a minute. Are you saying you don't know who those girls are?"

"Not a clue."

"Do the names Constance Marie and Linda Elizabeth ring any bells?"

Mac shook his head, and Hank folded his arms in front of him.

"How about Wendell Estates Wines?"

Mac swallowed hard. "Those girls are heiresses?"

"Big money, my friend. Super big bucks. And just look at you!" He slapped Mac's arm. "Already making inroads."

"It's not anything like that. You've got it all wrong."

"Have I? Last time I saw you, you were pretty down on your luck. Penniless, actually. Then, clear out of the sky, the great gods deliver. Not one goddess, but two!"

"One of them's married."

"Perfect. That means one of them's not."

"You're not much of a doctor." He shifted with a grimace, extending his leg. "You haven't even taken a look at this."

"Right you are." Hank slipped on his glasses and tucked up Mac's pants leg. He paused, lifting his eyes to Mac's. "I'm not saying you have to marry her. Just be all friendly like. Maybe her family will take pity on you. Invest in your new store."

"Nobody takes pity on me." He stiffened at the offense. "I do plenty fine looking after myself."

"Sure you do." Hank gingerly fingered his ankle, and Mac winced. "Anything else hurt?"

"Everything else hurts, but it's the ankle that bothers me the most."

Hank finished his examination, then rolled Mac's jeans leg back down. "Well, it will live," he said, patting his friend's knee. "Just keep some pressure and ice on it for the next couple of days. Oh yeah, and elevate it if you can."

Connie and Linda sat on a bench beneath a mounted bear head in the lobby.

"I hope he's all right," Connie said with concern.

"Yeah, me too. We leave for Napa in the morning." She turned toward her sister. "Are you sure you won't change your mind about…?"

"No! I'm telling you, Linda. That level of deception is against my moral code."

Just then, Connie's cell phone rang. She stared down at the incoming number with a gasp. Linda looked too, then said, "Well, look who it is. The old code breaker."

"Grandpa," Connie said, activating her speakerphone. "What a coincidence. We were just talking about you."

"And I was just thinking about you," he said with a wheeze. "You and Linda both. Of course, there *is* one major difference between you." He broke into a sporadic coughing fit, then caught his breath. "*She's* my married granddaughter." Connie could just imagine him sitting there in an expensive bathroom and in his high-end electric wheelchair. Several beautiful nurses were bound to be catering to him as they spoke. One combing his silvery hair. Another straightening the pillow at his back. A third sweetly bringing him a tray laid for tea. "But not for long, eh?" he continued. "Soon, you'll be next. Then all of the Oliver women will have fulfilled the family tradition."

Linda met her gaze, and Connie frowned.

"The tradition," the old man went on, "that your grandmother began. One dress made from original Paris lace, destined to bless an entire family. Every female in the lineage. And it's a good thing your blessed day is nearly here." He hacked loudly into his receiver. "I'm not getting any younger, you know. The doctors say I could go at any minute." Linda's brow creased with concern as Connie's heart hung heavy with worry. She loved her grandfather greatly. It was painful to imagine he wouldn't always be around. "I thank God every day you came to your senses and found yourself a groom before my eightieth birthday. What a gift this is to me. My very last granddaughter getting married! And just in the nick of time. You *are* bringing him to the party, eh? Just like you promised?"

"You promised to bring him to the party?" Linda spewed under her breath. "Why didn't you say so?"

She hadn't said so, because leaving out that little detail hadn't seemed worse than omitting all the rest of the truths she'd left unsaid. She really was in a horrible mess. Maybe she should come right out and say it. "Grandpa," she began tentatively, "the truth is, I have something to tell you…"

He choked up on the other end of the line, springing into another coughing and wheezing spell. "Hang on, dear granddaughter. Hold on." He breathed between fits and starts. "That's my Connie," she heard him tell one of the nurses. "The last single gal in the family. But she's going to do it before I die. Make me and her late grandmother proud." He started coughing again, and someone took away the phone.

"I'm afraid Mr. Oliver will have to call you back," a female voice said while the coughing continued.

"Of course," Connie said as Linda studied her with a sad look. "Oh, Linda," she said, feeling defeated. "What am I going to do? He may not even live until my imaginary wedding."

"He didn't sound good," Linda agreed.

Emotion roiled within Connie at the thought of losing her grandfather. He'd been more like a dad to her and her siblings than their real father had, always taking an interest in their lives, asking about and supporting their goals. It was only in advanced old age that he'd begun getting ornery, a little pigheaded perhaps, and intent on getting his way. But considering the constant love and support he'd provided the family throughout the years, everyone saw fit to indulge him. Even if that meant supplying him with three beautiful nurses, when one homely one would have been sufficient. "You don't know how I hate ruining his party. Especially thinking that..." Connie's eyes welled with tears.

Linda reached out and took her hand. "Then don't."

"I'm not taking some crazed, suicidal maniac back to Napa!"

"We're not sure he's suicidal. Why don't we see what the doctor says first?" Linda pulled a tissue from her pocket and handed it over.

"Sure, and then what?" Connie dabbed her eyes with a sniff.

"Well, if he's willing. I mean, wanting to make some money..."

Connie sat up a little straighter. "You're saying we should buy him?"

"*Rent him* is more like it. Just for the weekend. What do you say?"

The idea was ridiculous. Ludicrous. And yet it would keep her grandfather from knowing. At least for the next little while, until he got past his eightieth birthday. "But Grandpa thinks I'm marrying Walt!"

"That doesn't matter. You just say that Walt got away and you found a new one. A better one. An environmentalist." Her voice rose with excitement. "That's got a ring to it!"

Connie cocked her head, considering this. *An environmentalist with a beard. Hmm.*

Linda clasped her hands together, gaining more enthusiasm as she spoke. "He seems intelligent, well-spoken. Plus, he *is* rather handsome. You admitted it yourself. And, *ooh*, this is the best part. You can say that he saved you!"

"Saved me?"

"That's how you met."

"But Linda, he nearly killed me! Fell right down on top of me!"

"Details." Linda held her gaze. "You've got to look at the big picture. And, at the end of the day, he saved us both from a fate worse than... I don't know...coyotes."

"Or grizzlies."

"Snakes even!"

"Spiders."

"All of it. Absolutely."

"But we can't say we met this weekend and got engaged already."

"We'll claim we came hiking before. That you and he have been an item for weeks."

Oh, what a tangled web we weave, Connie thought, heaving a sigh. "What makes you think he'll do it?"

"What's the cash advance limit on your credit card? With mine, we'll double it."

"You think we can do this and not get caught? Not even by..." She thumbed heavenward. "You know."

"Oh, God already knows, and He approves."

"What?"

"Lies are only bad when they're told for selfish reasons, meant to hurt other people. This little...*thing*...we're talking here? It's like playacting, a harmless charade that will help Grandpa go to his grave in peace."

This still didn't feel right to Connie, but she couldn't think of another way out of the horrible corner she'd painted herself into. Would it really be so wrong to bring a handsome friend home for the party? Help everyone get through the weekend intact without causing a big scene with her melodramatic news: *Constance Marie Oliver has lost—yet another—groom.*

Just then, the door to Hank's office opened, and the two men emerged.

"Is he going to be all right?" Linda asked with concern.

"Oh yes, he'll be just fine. Ankle's merely twisted. Nothing's broken," Hank said. "And that other small concern you had?" He made a tugging motion beside his throat like he was yanking on a rope. "All a big misunderstanding."

Connie breathed a sigh of relief. "Really?"

Mac gave her a tilted grin, and her heart fluttered. "Totally," he said, appearing amused. "Facts are, I was up in that tree fully intending to stow my grub for the night. To keep it away from bears."

"Bears, you see?" Linda said, elbowing her. "I told you there was a logical explanation. Connie glared at her sister, knowing she'd said no such thing.

Connie pursed her lips a beat, then asked tentatively, "Maybe he should still have his head examined?"

"You're right on that." Hank snapped his fingers. "Already gave the guys at the clinic a call. They're expecting you."

"Us?" Connie asked with surprise.

"Until we're sure there's no brain swelling, it's probably best if Mac doesn't drive. I'd take him myself, but I can't leave things unmanned here." He glanced at Linda, then met Connie's eyes. "You don't mind?"

A few hours later, Mac approached the girls in the clinic waiting room, waving a stack of papers. They stood to greet him as he drew near.

"Tests all came back negative. Doctors say I'm fine."

"Other than your ankle?" Connie asked.

"Already feeling better." He shot her a smile. "After the X-rays, they rewrapped it pretty well. Said ice it for a day. Keep it stable. Before you know it, I'll be as good as new."

"That's great news, isn't it, Connie?" Linda asked.

"Really super." Connie swallowed hard and glanced at her sister. The whole time they'd sat in the waiting room, they'd been discussing their plans for bringing Mac back to Napa. They'd agreed in advance not to invite him if he received a negative doctor's report. Now that he was in the clear, there wasn't anything to stop Connie from asking. Other than levelheaded reason.

"Um, Mac," Linda said sweetly. "Connie here has something ask you."

"Oh?" He turned his handsome face toward hers, and Connie's cheeks flared.

This wouldn't be so bad, would it? Just a little bit of make-believe, for just a few days? "Um, yes," she said, feeling her voice falter. She collected her courage and strode toward Mac. "We... I...actually have somewhat of a business proposition."

"Business?" he asked, seeming mildly intrigued.

"It's my grandpa," she began uncertainly. Just how could she phrase it, other than blurting out the truth? She heard her voice crack as she said, "He's dying, Mac. Doesn't have much time left at all."

He studied her sympathetically. "I'm sorry, Connie. That must be terribly hard."

"Harder than you know." She met his gaze and felt lost in the depths of it. "He thinks... He wants..."

"Connie's supposed to be getting married," Linda filled in, growing impatient.

"You what?" Mac stared at her in surprise. "I didn't see any ring."

Connie's breath caught in her throat. "You were checking?"

"Wow," Linda murmured with delight.

"Wow," Connie echoed, still caught up in Mac's eyes.

"No ring?" He raised his brow with the question.

"Oh, that's because he... What I mean is, there's no groom. Not anymore."

Mac leaned forward, his voice husky. "What's your proposition?"

"I was hoping you'd do me a little favor."

"How little?"

"A weekend little."

"What's in it for me?"

"How much do you want?"

"Is this about money?"

"Is there anything else?"

"You tell me."

Of course there wasn't anything else. This was *all* about money, and buying time for her grandpa. That was all there was to it. Right?

"Maybe we should have a seat while I explain."

Chapter Four

The next morning, Mac found himself riding in the back of Linda's shiny new convertible, while the two sisters sat up front. He tried to convince himself he was doing this for a good cause, going along with Connie's plan. Basically, it was a win-win. He could help her spare disappointing her grandfather, plus he'd get the cash he needed for the down payment to rebuild his store. If it were all about him, he might feel guilty about accepting payment, but the fact was Mac donated ten percent of the proceeds from his shop to Homes for Humanity. When his business had gone ablaze, he hadn't been the only one to suffer. The steady flow of support he'd provided that local organization had dried up too. Before, he hadn't hoped to raise enough capital to rebuild until sometime next year. This unexpected opportunity with Connie would give him a chance to break ground sooner. That would prove a boon to the local homeless, and Mac was determined to see it through. He didn't consider himself much of an actor, but seriously. How hard could it be? All he had to do was walk into some huge mansion and convince Connie's family, and any assorted staff they had, that he was the Real McCoy. Mac swallowed hard, hoping he hadn't bitten off more than he could chew.

He caught Connie checking him out in the rearview mirror and self-consciously massaged his jaw. Once he'd opted in on the plan, he'd decided sprucing up was in order. He'd trimmed his beard and mustache and cleaned himself up nicely. Still, he wondered if what he'd done was enough. As an outdoorsy sort of guy,

Mac wasn't much into finery. He didn't even own a suit and tie. There wasn't much need for one in the circles where he traveled. Mostly because those involved sitting with groups of friends around a campfire, tossing back a brewskie or two, while discussing the next great way to save the world. He'd always hoped he'd find the sort of girl who could share that rugged lifestyle with him. Someone equally adventurous and just as comfortable in the great outdoors. Plainly, that wasn't going to be one of these two.

Mac was glad it was Connie who needed the groom instead of her sister. Not that Linda wasn't pretty as well. It was more like instinct told him he'd have a much easier time pretending with Connie. She was smart and funny, and there was something extra appealing about her. He couldn't quite put his finger on it, but it was there when the two of them were together. He'd never forget the panicked look in her eyes when she'd run straight into him in the woods during her late-night toilet expedition. She'd been half crazed with fear in a way that was unbearably cute. It was all he could do to keep from teasing her into believing there really *was* a predator in those woods. That would have given him an excuse to hold her longer. And something told Mac that keeping Connie's lean, athletic body pressed up against his for an extra moment more would have meant sheer pleasure. Mac imagined her pretty blue eyes gazing up at him as he brought his mouth to her kissable lips, then pulled himself up short. Per Connie's instruction, there was to be no kissing during these next few days. They had a business arrangement, pure and simple. All Mac was there to do was give the *illusion* of someone desperately interested in Connie.

And that was what he'd do too. Play the politely respectful fiancé, wow Connie's family, and convince her grandfather that he was Constance Oliver's one true love. Then he could go back to rebuilding his life, and Connie would find a way to carry on with hers. Despite his initial reservations, Mac was starting to believe that everything would work out fine. In a way, he was being a gentleman. Merely assisting a damsel in distress. So what if his help came with a price tag? When that cash could ultimately help so many people, charging for his time didn't seem all bad. Life wasn't perfect, and sometimes you had to make sacrifices in order to achieve your goals. Connie and he were in agreement on that.

Connie hoped Mac hadn't seen her peeking at him in her vanity mirror, but she thought he'd spied her looking just the same. She put on a dab of lipstick, then shut the mirror flap and flipped up her visor. Linda was right. If she hadn't been such a big chicken, Connie never would have gotten herself into this mess. But she'd been afraid of upsetting her whole family's plans, and most particularly of breaking her grandpa's heart. His health was failing, and she didn't know how well he could withstand another emotional blow. When she'd lost her last fiancé, her grandpa had been hospitalized a whole week! She'd gone to visit and had overheard him begging the priest, *"Please ask God to let me live long enough to see my last granddaughter married."* On one hand, Connie had felt upset his expectations put so much pressure on her. On the other, she understood he came from a traditional background where he wanted to feel as if the women in the family were taken care of. Naturally, Connie could take care of herself. But at nearly eighty years old, her grandfather couldn't be convinced. There wasn't much point in trying.

Connie sighed and looked out at the rolling hills around them. They'd be approaching their vineyard soon. Linda hadn't said much during their long drive. She'd just sat there wearing dark glasses, with that baseball cap on her head and the radio turned up high, blasting out some funky Brazilian tunes. She didn't appear to be having second thoughts about their plan. In fact, she seemed uncannily relaxed, sitting there thumping her fingers against the steering wheel to the beat of the music, a mildly distracted expression on her face. She was probably thinking about Beau and being back in his arms. They had such a great marriage, those two. It was a hard enough act to follow with a genuine fiancé. Connie wasn't one hundred percent sure she'd be able to pull it off with a fake one. She'd have to try, though. Her grandpa's happiness during his big birthday celebration depended on it. The deal she'd struck with Mac would ultimately help a lot of other people too. How hard could it be? Pretending she was about to get married? She'd played that role three times already. By now, she should have it down pat.

Mac had to keep his jaw from dropping when they pulled up the broad circular drive. No sooner had they arrived under the huge portico when three staff members popped outdoors. A valet went immediately to the driver's side, ushering Linda out of the car, while two others elegantly opened car doors for Connie and Mac, offering to assist with luggage. Mac didn't have much except for the rucksack he'd slung in the trunk, and he was capable of carrying that himself. Likely much more capable than the slender, elderly man who offered to take it for him. Mac was floored. He didn't think people really had butlers anymore. At least they didn't in the neighborhood he came from. He stared up at the peach-colored house, styled somewhat like an Italian villa, and counted ten sets of windows across, and that was on *either side* of the looming front door. The upstairs appeared even grander, with pretty balconies protruding from french doors that swept across the building's stucco façade.

Connie and Linda chatted easily with the old man, who Connie introduced as Charles, and the sweet middle-aged lady named Matilda who fussed over the girls, telling them how well they looked after their time out "in nature." Neither seemed to miss a beat when Connie claimed him as her fiancé. Each had simply given him a cursory once-over and said they hoped he'd enjoy his stay. In an odd sort of way, Mac's appearance seemed fairly routine to them. Mac secretly wondered just how many other fiancés Connie had previously brought home, then decided he'd better not ask. As the valet drove the car away, the front door swung open before they could reach it.

"Darlings!" an elegant fifty-something woman said. She was neatly put together with a soft complexion and yellow-gold hair spun up in a twist.

"Hi, Mom," the girls said in turn, giving her quick hugs.

"I heard you come through the front gate, and—" She turned her gaze suddenly on Mac. "Well, hello. Who do we have here?"

Matilda and Charles stepped past her, carting the girls' luggage up a curved staircase. The stunning entrance hall was plastered with works of art and dripping with elegant chandeliers. Through archways beyond it, Mac spied more staff members setting up dining tables draped with white linen cloths in a central courtyard plumed with potted plants and flowers. Silverware clanked lightly as place settings were laid around blooming centerpieces.

"Mother," Connie said, proudly taking his arm. "I'd like you to meet Mac, my fiancé."

"Your...? I'm sorry, did you say *fiancé*?"

Connie nodded triumphantly, and their mom leaned toward Linda with a whisper. "What happened to...?" she asked, but not quite quietly enough.

Connie waved her free hand in the air. "Ancient history, but this man, here..." She tugged Mac toward her by their interlinked arms. "*He* is my future."

"Oh my." She looked back and forth between the two of them, her aristocratic cheekbones turning a dusty rose. "Well, Mac," she said, collecting herself. "It's very nice to meet you." She extended her hand. "I'm Elizabeth Oliver. Welcome to our home."

"I thought I heard chatter!" A middle-aged man with salt-and-pepper hair drew near, appearing from the west wing. "Linda, Constance, welcome back." He curiously eyed Mac. "Greetings."

"Mac's the *fiancé*," Elizabeth said with a tight smile.

The color drained from his face. "The what?"

Connie extended the fingers of her left hand, flashing him a lovely solitaire. She and Linda had agreed she couldn't surface with a fake fiancé and no ring. It had been a simple matter of sliding the one back on her finger that Walt had given her. Since he'd refused to take it back, she hadn't even removed it until the morning of their hiking excursion. It was practically like an old friend, having spent barely any time off her finger at all. Elizabeth raised an eyebrow and stared at Connie.

"You and I need to talk," she said, forcing out words lined with sugar.

"Sure, Mom," Connie said brightly. "Just as soon as Mac settles in."

"Mac," her father said with an appraising frown, "I'm Wendell Jr., but calling me Mr. Oliver will work fine."

Mac nodded. "Thank you for including me in your family's celebration."

"Why, you're practically family too." Elizabeth demurely cocked her chin. "Aren't you?"

Connie loudly shut the front door behind her as a younger man bounded down the steps. He appeared to be in his twenties with a solid build and dark hair like his father's.

"Well, look who's home!" he bellowed. "My two favorite sisters in the world."

"We're your only two sisters," Linda replied smartly before making her departure. "If you guys will excuse me," she told the others, "I have a husband to find."

Connie's brother strode over and took Mac's hand. "You must be Connie's intended. I'm Ollie."

"Adam McCormack, but my friends call me Mac." He shook Ollie's hand. "Good to know you."

"Ollie?" Elizabeth said in her gracious-hostess tone, why don't you show Mac to the blue room upstairs while I help Connie unpack?"

"No problem. Can I help you with that?" he asked, referencing Mac's backpack.

"Thanks. I've got it," Mac said, hoping his eyes didn't betray him as he looked around. This place was a palace, nearly as large as a museum. Heck, maybe it was even bigger than some of them. The real difference was, when showtime came, Mac was well aware that he'd be the one on display.

"What's going on?" Elizabeth asked as Connie unpacked her bags.

Connie turned her back on her mom to hang a few things in her closet. "Like I told you, Mac is my fiancé. We're engaged."

"Since when?"

Connie paused in sliding her cotton shirt onto a hanger. She hadn't had occasion to use all her clothes. Being lost in the forest had spared some of her wardrobe. "Since...he asked me to marry him!" Having her mom believe in the charade was just as important as convincing her grandfather. It was *one for all, and all for one* in this family. If her folks didn't buy in, her Grandpa might grow skeptical too.

Her mom strode over and leaned into the door jamb of the closet. She stared straight at Connie, who stood there with that blasted hanger hovering in midair. "And, when was that? Precisely?"

"Um..." Connie hooked the hanger over the closet bar and quickly tried to calculate a reasonable date. But it was hard to focus on a mental calendar with her mom trapping her in that cool blue stare. "It was shortly after Walt dumped me," she added hastily before hurrying back to her suitcase to grab another armful of clothes. "At first I worried it was a rebound thing. But nope! We're solid."

"Gracious. That's all clean? Didn't you wear anything while you were gone?" Suddenly seeming to recall her daughter had been with Mac, Elizabeth bit her lip. "Don't tell me you and he... Not with Linda along!"

"For heaven's sake, Mom. You know me better than that. Besides, it's not like Linda's a saint, you know."

A few bedrooms away and just down the hall, Linda drew the curtains, hearing the shower running. It had been too long since she'd seen him; she couldn't wait. Beau was her everything. Her sun and the moon, with a nice smattering of stardust too. She'd been so lucky to find him, and now she was eager to remind him how happy she felt. She slipped from her clothes and laid her hand on the bathroom doorknob, turning it gently. Every room in this house was its own master suite, complete with a well-appointed bath. While she didn't live here anymore, she could still appreciate the amenities this house had to offer.

Not that she minded the cute bungalow she shared with Beau in the city. She found it charming, in fact, and had worked hard to make their small house feel like a home. Beau worked hard too, toiling relentlessly in medical school. She couldn't be any more proud of him, or any more determined to help support his dream by keeping things together on her accountant's salary. Linda had always been good with numbers and was proud of what she did. She also was infinitely pleased that she and Beau were getting by without any help from her exceedingly wealthy family. He had a part-time job in the lab, and together they were making it. Once he had passed his boards and begun practicing, they'd be better off still. Linda sneaked into the bathroom, thinking how much she loved her life.

The room was steamy and warm, the full length of the mirror fogged with steam. Repressing a giggle, she pressed open the double shower door and stepped inside.

"Who's there?" Beau asked, still lathering his hair.

She wrapped her arms around him, her forearms slipping against his hairy, muscled chest. "Who do you think?" she asked above the rush of the water.

He rubbed the lather from his eyes and spun slowly to face her in the steamy downpour. "I was hoping to hell it was my wife," he said, his voice husky.

She looked up at him, thrilled to be his, wanting to be all his for the moment.

"Who else would it be?" she asked saucily, sliding her arms up his back and linking her hands behind his neck.

"Matilda?" he teased with a grin.

She laughed happily. "Stop it!"

"Stop?" he said, pulling her to him and bringing his mouth down on hers. "I was just about to start."

"Did you bring any other clothes?" Ollie asked as Mac dumped the contents of his rucksack on the bed.

"What you see is what you get."

"Hmm."

"I hope it's not a problem. In my day job, I don't have much occasion to—"

"What is your day job, by the way?"

"I run a camping store. Did, I mean."

"Did?"

"Got roasted in that last round of forest fires."

Ollie's face registered sympathy. "I'm sorry. That's rough."

"Some things can't be helped. Acts of God."

"Or nature."

"No."

Ollie studied him, appraising his frame. "Tell you what, I might have something that will work."

"A suit, you mean?"

Ollie shrugged. "We always dress for dinner here, and Grandpa's party will be no exception. No offense, but jeans and flannel probably won't cut it."

"No offense taken," Mac answered honestly, feeling as if Connie should have warned him. Then again, maybe she hadn't thought of it herself. They were so busy concocting their imaginary backstory, they'd completely failed to talk about what each of them should wear. Of course, Connie always came out well-coiffed. So maybe it hadn't even occurred to her that Mac might require a few gentle suggestions.

"Be back in a sec," Ollie said with a grin.

"Speaking of clothing," Elizabeth said, "we've had a very special arrival from New York this week."

Connie caught her breath with a gasp. "The dress?"

"*The dress,*" her mom answered with a firm nod. "And let me tell you it is *beau-ti-ful*. Just gorgeous. That heirloom storage shop does impeccable work."

Connie swallowed hard. "I'm sure." She walked in a daze to the bed and sat with a thunk. Naturally, her mom and the rest of the family had still supposed she was marrying Walt in a few months, but nobody had warned her the historic wedding gown was being recalled from storage already. "What's the rush?"

Elizabeth sat beside her, giving her a sympathetic smile. "The *rush*, darling, is that you had a wedding planned for August. Dresses require fittings. Even one as special as this, with which your grandmother took such care." And her Grandma Oliver had taken great care too. She'd thought out the entire process of her dress being passed down to her daughters in advance. In case they were larger than she was, she'd had an extra panel made from matching Paris lace, which could be inserted in back to augment the dress. In the event they were taller, she'd had an additional underskirt made, also from identical Paris lace, which could increase the gown's length. But alas, after all that trouble, she and Wendell Oliver, Senior had only been blessed with three boys. Fortunately for the intended family tradition, each of them had produced wives and daughters, with Wendell Junior delivering two girls of his own. After her mom and a preceding line of aunts and cousins, Linda had worn the dress and looked lovely. It was Connie's turn to wear it next. Their grandpa was firmly convinced that the dress held great magical powers to bestow a happy marriage. Well, it seemed to have worked out in Linda's case anyhow.

"Don't worry, love. No one will expect an August wedding to go off with your recent change in plans. But the happy part is now we're planning for a new one. Probably not too much further away."

"Actually, Mac and I were thinking of having a very long engage—"

"Nonsense! The dress is already here, and we've gotten so much initial planning done. It might take some tweaking here and there, but I'm sure once we pin down a new date—*for your new man*," Elizabeth added with a wink, "we'll set everything in order."

Connie met her gaze. "I know. But wouldn't it be great if... Just for this weekend? We could focus on Grandpa and his party?"

Elizabeth warmly patted her hand. "Of course, you're right. But before I leave you to get ready, do tell me more about Mac. I'm dying to know how you met. And Walt...? Oh my," she said with a serious frown. "What on earth happened there?" She studied her daughter's finger. "And why are you still wearing his ring?"

Connie gulped. "Um. The one from Mac is on order. He's having it custom-made."

"And he's okay with this...substitution?"

"Oh yeah, totally fine. Mac's what you'd call a super chill guy."

Ollie slid his charcoal Armani suit jacket onto Mac's back. "It may be a little snug in the shoulders, but you can make do."

Mac squirmed uncomfortably, feeling as if he'd been pinned in something akin to a straitjacket. "Thanks, Ollie. Very nice of you to do this."

Ollie adjusted Mac's tie, then stepped aside so he could view himself in the mirror. He looked okay, he supposed. He just wasn't used to it. The trousers fit awfully tight too and were a tad short at the ankles. Didn't help matters that Mac had brought only his hiking boots. Doctor's orders. *"Keep those on the next few days,"* the doc had said. Perfect for providing extra stability.

"Don't suppose you brought any other shoes?" Ollie asked, looking down.

Mac shook his head.

"No worries." Ollie soundly slapped his shoulder. "No one will likely even notice."

Linda sidled up next to Connie as she sipped her champagne. "Did you reconnect with your husband?" Connie asked, lifting an eyebrow.

Linda shot her a devilish grin. "In a manner of speaking."

"Where is the lucky guy?"

"I sent him down the hall to introduce himself to Mac. You know, so the poor guy would have one more person in his corner."

Connie gasped. "You didn't tell him?"

"About the ruse? No way. That's just our sisters' secret."

Connie sighed with relief and raised her drink to her lips. The panorama before them was dotted with party guests, all dressed in finery and tilting champagne flutes as a Latin band played.

"Whose idea was the music?" Connie asked.

"Grandpa's, of course."

"I thought he'd given up salsa dancing?"

Linda turned toward her. "I wouldn't put it past him to try it in a wheelchair. Not if he could convince one of those pretty nurses to sit on his lap."

Connie giggled briefly, but then grew serious. "Do you think Mom suspects?"

"Why would you say that?"

"I don't know. I just get a funny feeling."

"Maybe you shouldn't have flashed that rock the way you did." Linda angled her head toward Connie's left hand.

"But you swore nobody would notice!"

"That it's the one Walt gave you? Nobody might have! Unless you'd put it on such proud display."

"Well, when Dad asked—"

"Shh," Linda cautioned quietly. "It's Grandpa. He's coming."

The crowd broke into applause as the old man wheeled into the courtyard, escorted by two lovely caretakers. One brunette and one blonde.

Just then, Mac and Beau approached the sisters, who stood beside a potted fern.

"Connie," Beau acknowledged with a nod of his head. "Good to see you. You look lovely."

And she did too. Her beauty nearly took Mac's breath away. She was gorgeous in a short blue dress that complemented the color of her eyes. And the heels she was wearing did everything to accentuate the curves of her lovely legs.

"Thanks, Beau," she said, giving him a peck on the cheek. "Love the tie."

But Mac was so caught up in Connie, he couldn't even recall what color Beau's tie was. Red? No. Yellow? He didn't dare chance a look if that meant breaking away from Connie's gaze. She looked like a princess, regal somehow. With that neat string of pearls around her neck and the tasteful dangling earrings to match. This Constance Oliver was one uptown woman. And Mac was nothing but a down-home guy, he reminded himself as his shoulder blades twitched beneath the jacket's tight constraints.

"Wow, you're just gorgeous." Realizing his mistake, he turned his attention immediately on Linda. "Both of you ladies are knockouts for sure."

Linda smiled and said something to Beau, while Connie's face colored sweetly. "Thanks," she told Mac. "You look great too." Suddenly her gaze dropped to the floor. "Are those hiking boots?" She looked up again.

"It's all he had," Ollie explained, surfacing with three flutes of champagne, one for himself and the rest for the other two gentlemen.

The small group watched as Elizabeth and Wendell Junior walked into the courtyard to stand proudly beside Wendell Senior's wheelchair. "Ladies and gentlemen," Wendell Junior said in his best booming voice. "May I present...the birthday boy!"

People clapped and cheered as Connie's grandpa did a small pirouette in his wheelchair, grinning broadly.

"I thought he was very ill?" Mac whispered to Connie.

"It comes and goes," she whispered back.

"You'll see what she means," Linda added.

To Mac's surprise, Elizabeth silenced the crowd with her celebratory pronouncement. "And now, in keeping with the way in which *the birthday boy* likes to run his parties, let's all have a little cake and ice cream!"

"Granddad always has dessert before dinner on his birthday," Ollie explained. "He figures it's the one day he can do what he wants."

"Yeah, and all of the rest of us get to join him," Beau quipped.

Linda elbowed her husband. "Be nice. You know you enjoy having the cake first just as much as he does. Besides, nobody's *forced* to eat it. You can always save yours for later."

Before Mac knew it, a huge, tiered cake was being rolled out onto the floor on a movable table. Rather than having candles on top, it was adorned by dozens of dancing sparklers, hissing merrily with all their might beneath a rousing chorus of "Happy Birthday." Grandpa Oliver's face lit up in a big, broad smile as he plucked a sparkler off the cake and began waving it around like a maestro directing his orchestra, just in time to conduct the crowd in singing "For He's A Jolly Good Fellow."

Then, halfway through the second chorus, the old man glanced their way, staring straight at Connie. Within seconds, he'd doubled over, dropping his sparkler to the floor and breaking into a prolonged coughing fit. The room fell silent as nurses scrambled to assist him. Elizabeth dug in her purse for her smartphone, preparing to call 9-1-1. Connie and Linda were about to rush forward when their grandpa slowly raised his right hand, bringing himself under control.

"I'm all right," he told his worried daughter-in-law before glancing once again at Connie. "For now."

Mac pulled the handkerchief that Ollie had loaned him from his pocket to wipe his brow. And he thought there was excitement in the wild. None of his adventures in the great outdoors had anything on this.

Linda turned toward Mac with a knowing look. "See what I mean?" she asked.

Mac tucked away his hanky and took another sip of champagne. "I think I'm starting to get it."

"Come on," Connie told him. "It's time you met my grandfather."

"You mean right now?"

"No time like the present," she said, tugging him forward.

Mac didn't know why he felt nervous about meeting the octogenarian, but somehow the looming encounter set him slightly on edge. Maybe it was those inward seeds of guilt about deceiving this family that had bloomed the moment he'd stepped through the palatial front door. Or maybe it was the scowl on the old man's face as he lowered his dark-rimmed glasses and appraised Mac with a frown.

"Grandpa!" Connie proclaimed, leaning down to plant a kiss on his head while she squeezed his shoulders in a hug. "You don't look a day over sixty."

He coughed once into his balled-up fist. "I wish I felt that on the inside."

Connie grabbed the handles of his wheelchair and pivoted him toward Mac. "I'd like you to meet my new fiancé, Mac."

Grandpa hacked again. "*New fiancé?* What happened to the old one?"

Connie hung her head. "He got away," she said softly.

"Speak up, granddaughter! Can't hear you above the commotion!"

The band played on as servers bustled about the room, depositing cake and ice cream at the various place settings.

"I said, Walt left me!" she shouted louder.

Wendell Senior raised his brow. "Left you? What a dolt that one was." He gave a dismissive wave of his hand. "Never liked him anyway." He turned his eyes on Mac and studied him from the top of his hairy head all the way down the too-tight lines of his suit and landing at his hiking boots. "Hmm," he said, adjusting his glasses to get a better look. "Uh-hum." He returned his gaze to Mac's. "And just what is it that you do, young man?"

"Well, sir, I—"

"He runs his own business," Connie shared.

Mac glanced at her, then continued to address Wendell Senior. "Yes, sir, a camping store. I mean, I did. That was before it—"

"You don't need to bore Grandpa with the details," Connie chirped.

"Did he say *camping store*?" Grandpa asked before making a show of trying to clean out his ears. He set his steely gray eyes on Mac. "You mean you do this part-time while you're in school or something? A graduate program, perhaps?"

"No, sir. That's what I do full-time. Would if—"

"He's very good at it too," Connie inserted proudly. "Charitable, besides. Can you believe Mac gives ten percent of his proceeds to the indigent?"

"Is that why he dresses like them?"

"Grandpa!"

Mac felt his temperature spike. Now he didn't know much, but he could tell when he was being insulted. "I think I'll just go refill our champagne," he said to Connie, retrieving the empty flute from her hand.

As he departed, Connie turned angry eyes on her grandfather. "That wasn't very nice, and you know it."

"What's our loveable old grandpa done now?" Linda asked, approaching.

"He just told Mac he looked like a homeless person."

"That wasn't very welcoming."

Wendell Senior motioned toward Mac as he strode away, his clothes nearly bursting at the seams. "Well, just look at him! With that ill-fitting outfit and that hairy monkey mug. He looks like he swings from the trees!"

"Tried but failed," Linda said under her breath.

Connie shot her a silencing look, then met her grandpa's eyes. "Mac really is a very nice man. I wish you'd give him a chance."

"But how did all this happen? The first thing I know, you're engaged to that nice young attorney, Walt…"

"You were just saying you never liked him!"

"That was before."

"Before what?"

"Before I realized you'd tossed him over for Tarzan."

"Tarzan never had a beard," Linda added unhelpfully.

"He is *not* Tarzan. But Mac is a very skilled outdoorsman. He saved my life. Both of ours, in fact. Didn't he, Linda?"

Their granddad surveyed Linda doubtfully. Connie nudged her.

"It's true!" Linda spouted. "That's how he and Connie met. We went hiking."

"Got lost in the woods," Connie said.

"Could have been there for days."

"Weeks even."

"Eaten alive by bears."

Wendell Senior motioned across the room. "And that man over there—spilling champagne on his hiking boots—saved you?"

"Yes," both girls said together.

"Harrumph." He cocked his chin sideways and appeared to be considering something. "Didn't you girls just get back from the wilderness?"

Linda rushed in. "Yes, but she met Mac weeks ago."

"This last trip was our second one."

"You've only seen the man twice and you're engaged?"

"Heavens, no." Connie gave a little giggle like that was the most ridiculous thing she'd heard. "We've been dating for weeks."

"Where?"

"There!" Linda said, overlapping with Connie's words. "Here! In Napa!"

Grandpa Oliver narrowed his gaze. "Here, there, and…everywhere?"

"It's been on the computer," Connie said, thinking quickly.

Linda didn't miss a beat. "That's right. Internet dating. I'm sure you've heard of it. It's really big right now."

Wendell Senior studied both their faces. "And people get engaged this way?"

"All the time," Connie said.

"Well, maybe if you'd dated him in person, you could have given him some tips on his wardrobe."

Mac returned with their champagne just in time for Connie to make their excuses and retreat from her grandfather. She didn't know why he'd been so tough on Mac. It really wasn't fair to judge him by his occupation…or appearance…or dress code. She sighed inwardly, knowing that was just the Oliver way. She accepted the flute Mac handed her with a grateful smile.

"Thanks. I was just telling Grandpa we were about to take our seats for cake and ice cream."

"Sir," Mac said politely. "It was very nice meeting you."

Wendell Senior twisted his lips and remained silent until Linda pinched him. "Ow!" He gave Linda a cursory glance, then returned his gaze to Mac's. "And it was a…" He seemed to be struggling with the words. "…pleasure meeting you as well. I hope that you'll enjoy the party."

Chapter Five

Thankfully for Mac, the meal portion of the evening passed a lot more pleasantly. They were seated at a table with Linda and her gregarious husband, Beau, as well as Ollie and his girlfriend, Trudy. Trudy had come in late, rushing over from her stint as an intern at a local television station. She hoped to work in broadcast news someday and had the pretty face and nicely even-toned voice to carry off being an anchorwoman. He learned that Ollie had gained entry into a prestigious film production master's program near Los Angeles, and that Linda was an accountant and Beau was in medical school. The Olivers were one incredibly ambitious and educated family. On the way here, he'd learned that Connie was still figuring out what she wanted to do. While she'd majored in studio art with a concentration in photography in college, she'd never quite found the fit for her art. More than anything, she loved to photograph food, which Mac found both quirky and charming. Linda had assured him that Connie was also a fabulous baker. She made the most wonderful cakes and pies, very detailed too. She'd even styled a cake like a human brain for Beau's birthday when he'd been studying anatomy, complete with a prefrontal lobe and all. Since she'd not yet found a market for her competing and unusual talents, Connie worked as a docent at a children's museum in order to pay her bills.

Especially after seeing the lavish lifestyle she'd come from, Mac couldn't imagine Connie having difficulty with finances. He found it admirable she aspired to stand on her own two feet, even though she'd unmistakably come from money. All of the Oliver children appeared to share that trait. Elizabeth and Wendell Junior must have done something right. In Mac's case, he'd never considered that he had any option other than forging out on his own. He'd grown up with a hardworking yet loving single mother who'd worked double shifts at the bakery to pay for school extras so he could stay enrolled in the most competitive courses. Her support and his own dedication had paid off by landing him a full scholarship to the forestry program at Berkeley. Mac had never wanted to do anything but work outdoors. He'd initially considered working for the National Park Service but ultimately found running his own business—and being his own boss—to be the perfect fit. That was until everything went up in smoke.

His dinner plate was cleared and a flaming dish was placed before him. "Bananas Foster," Connie explained with a sweet smile. Mac couldn't believe they were serving dessert again. Not after having cake and champagne as appetizers… then a summer squash bisque *to start*… followed by the apple, pecan, and goat-cheese salad… wrapping up with prime rib and lobster…

"I don't know how you girls can eat like this and still keep your figures."

"StairMaster," Linda assured him with a grin.

Connie nodded in agreement, eagerly digging into her second dessert, but Mac didn't believe he could fit in one more bite. Already, he was bursting at the seams, particularly in this too-tight jacket. A server came around with coffee as the band picked up its tempo. The music was saucy and upbeat, and Connie must have liked it. He could hear her tapping her feet in time to the rhythm under the table. Wendell Junior silenced the band and took his place center stage. "Honored guests, friends, and family, we're delighted you could join us tonight for my father's very special celebration. And in honor of the man of the hour, I hope you'll all fulfill his request to dance until your shoes fall off." A ripple of laughter erupted from the crowd as Grandpa Oliver watched, beaming, from the sidelines. He motioned for his son to hand him the microphone, then took it to address the room.

"It was very kind of you to come this evening. Very kind of all of you, indeed. And I can't thank you enough for your donations to my chosen charities. The art museum and community playhouse will both benefit greatly from your generosity, and will hopefully keep entertaining others long past the time this old man is gone." As if to prove his frailty, he broke into a wheezing cough. Elizabeth appeared and took the microphone while Grandpa Oliver continued to breathe hoarsely. "Thank you. Thank you all again."

He beckoned Elizabeth toward him and whispered something in her ear as she held the microphone at her side. She brought the cordless mike to her mouth and her face warmed in a smile. "The birthday boy has a special request. Before we begin the general dancing, he'd like to welcome Connie's new fiancé to the fold with a special introductory couple's dance."

Mac's coffee sloshed sideways as he rapidly set his cup down on its saucer.

"Ladies and gentleman," Elizabeth went on, "may I present to you our daughter Connie's newly betrothed, Adam 'Mac' McCormack." She gestured grandly in his direction, and people applauded. Mac wanted to crawl under the table, but Connie stopped him by taking his hand.

"I can't dance," he whispered to her, his pulse picking up a notch.

"Of course you can," she said with a smile.

Mac heard cups clattering against saucers and dessert forks scraping dishes as Connie led him toward the center of the room. Was it his imagination, or were people actually whispering behind their hands about his boots?

Wendell Junior gave a signal to the bandleader, and the quartet began to play something with a lot of swing and dip. Mac had no clue what he was doing, so he let Connie lead as she pulled him along. Soon he was following her example, rocking back and forth and stepping sideways to the beat, all the while holding Connie's hand. He didn't know how she made it look so easy as she moved gracefully to the music, employing that seductive sway to her hips. Suddenly she eased forward, and Mac realized he was supposed to lift his arm so she could pass underneath. The moment he did, he felt something pop behind his right arm. The next thing he knew, Connie was passing behind him and circling around on the left, taking that hand and yanking back hard as she stepped out in front. *Rip.* Mac was sure he'd heard it, another seam tearing in his jacket. He hoped no one would notice, because there was no stopping Connie now. She was alive with the beat, her sweet face pink with exertion. Or maybe it was perspiration. Her pearl necklace bobbed in time to the music. *Swish.* She flung him forward, then pulled him back with both hands, tugging him up against her, as threads gave way in the seat of his pants. He had to say something, get her to stop. But then Elizabeth saved the moment by urging the rest of the guests onto the floor.

Once they were surrounded by a sea of gyrating bodies, Mac forgot all about his failing wardrobe. All he could think of was Connie, with her gorgeous blue eyes and that beautiful smile on her lips. Any man who'd walked away from her must have been an idiot. She was lively and fun and— *Holy Cow*, he thought as she spun him around again—built to last! Suddenly, Mac realized the music had stopped, and he had Connie pressed right up against him as she wound her arms around his back. Party guests clapped and oohed and aahed at the lovely couple, knitted closely together on the dance floor.

Out of nowhere, a chorus erupted. "Kiss, kiss, kiss!" The crowd became more and more insistent, cheering and clanking goblets with silver spoons.

Connie gazed up at him, her cheeks bright red. "We don't have to."

But if that was how she felt, why was there expectation in her eyes? Mac had seen that look in a woman before, and he knew exactly what it meant. It meant she wanted him to, oh yes, she did. And boy, in the heat of this crazy moment, didn't he want her too. Mac lowered his mouth to hers, unable to fight its magnetic pull, as the crowd raged on, hooting and hollering as their lips drew closer. Mac cradled her head in his hands, enjoying the silken feel of her hair while his mouth hovered over hers.

"Mac," she breathed, panting lightly. "Don't...stop."

And he didn't. He laid it on with all he had as people cheered and clinked glasses around them in celebration. And man, didn't her mouth taste good, all sweet and sugary like… Wait a minute. Bananas Foster? No sooner had that thought hit when a cold blast of air assaulted his bottom. Mac pulled back in shock to see his trousers had slid down to his ankles, and both of his jacket sleeves had popped off!

"Wow," he heard an older woman say from nearby. "Does she have that effect on *all* her fiancés?"

Chapter Six

Mac heard a knock at his door and cracked it open.

"Are you all right?" Connie asked with a worried look. She was still in her nice dress and pearls, looking as beautiful as ever. After his extremely embarrassing moment, Mac had hustled to his room to change back into his flannel shirt and jeans and hadn't resurfaced since. Despite the dancing, his ankle seemed relatively back to normal, so he'd dispensed with the ace bandage and dropped it in his pack. He'd since heard car doors popping open and vehicles driving away, so figured most of the guests had left by now.

"I'm sorry about what happened," he said. "Downstairs, I mean."

"That wasn't your fault."

"I'm glad you understand."

She brought her hand to her mouth to disguise a giggle. "You have to admit, it *was* kind of funny."

"Funny?"

"Oh, Mac," she said with a teasing lilt. "Nobody holds it against you that you did a striptease in front of the family. In fact, I think some of the older ladies kind of liked it."

He raised an eyebrow and met her eyes with a challenge. "Did *you* like it, Connie?"

She blushed suddenly. "Well, I... The truth is, I wasn't looking."

The heck she wasn't. Mac had seen her looking, all right. Ogling was more like it. And from the look in her eyes, she'd liked what she'd seen. "I can show you again, if you'd like to make sure…?" He brought a hand to the waist of his jeans, resting it on his belt.

She blinked hard and stepped back. "Oh no. That won't be necessary."

"Well, there you two are," Elizabeth said, striding toward them down the long hall. "Mac," she said, addressing him. "I hope you're feeling better. In the Oliver house, crazy things happen. Nobody will even remember by morning."

"Thanks. That's very gracious of you."

"Anyhow." Elizabeth clapped her hands together and gave them each a delighted look. "I have just the right thing to lighten the moment." She turned toward Mac. "I'm sure Connie's filled you in on the family's traditional wedding gown?"

"Yes, she has," he answered honestly.

"Then maybe it's time you saw it."

"Isn't that supposed to be bad luck before the wedding?"

"Only when it's on the bride," Elizabeth said with a smile.

Elizabeth pressed open the door to the gold room, exposing an elegant wedding gown on a mannequin positioned near the curtained window. Nearby lamps bathed the delicate fabric in their glow. The dress was intricately cut and made of hand-sewn lace. It appeared to have once been snowy white but had faded slightly over time.

Century-old pearls swept down the train, which fanned out on the floor, shimmering in the soft light. Connie sighed in spite of herself. It really was a magical dress. Made more magical still by all of the incredible women who had worn it, including her own mother at Grandma Oliver's request. Since she hadn't had any daughters and Wendell Junior had been the son to marry first, her grandma has insisted Elizabeth wear the gown in order to begin the new tradition and bestow the dress with its second blessing, bearing witness to another union blessed by God.

"Lovely, isn't it?" Elizabeth asked Mac. "I'm sure Connie has told you it's been in our family for years. Grandpa Oliver's wife Melissa wore it first, and then I did, as did the wives of my husband's two brothers. Each of the granddaughters has worn it too. That is…" She turned her eyes on her daughter. "All of them except for Connie. It's a joy to know that her turn is coming next."

"Next! Next!" A parrot squawked from a cage in the corner, startling Mac, who hadn't seen it earlier.

"Well, hey there, buddy," he told the big bird as it fluffed its feathers.

"Well, hey there, buddy!" the parrot answered.

"That's Gilbert," Elizabeth said with a laugh, "sentinel of the dress."

"Sentinel?" Mac questioned.

"Everyone takes dress security very seriously around here," Connie said. She hoisted a large volume off the dresser and handed it to him. "*The Book of Rules,*" she proclaimed with mock seriousness as the weight of it settled in Mac's hands.

The parrot squawked. "Book of Rules! Book of Rules!"

"Wow. Are you serious?" Mac asked the women.

"Oh yes," Elizabeth said, holding up a finger. "My sister-in-law Mona, who is the official guardian of the dress in New York, takes great care to see there are no infractions."

"That's because, in the past, there were," Connie explained. "Aunt Kara tried to hand-wash it rather than send it through the specialized service."

Elizabeth shook her head. "And this was after their Charleston home was hit by the hurricane."

"Hurricane?" Mac asked.

"The sleeves were horribly damaged," Connie confessed, "so we had to have a professional restyle it without them."

Elizabeth sighed. "Thus we now have rules…"

"The dress must go on over the head and never up over the hips," Connie said, as if reciting from memory.

Elizabeth held up her hand in a pledge. "No kneeling in the dress, even during a Catholic ceremony."

"And absolutely no dancing," Connie added with a stern shake of her head. "There are fines involved."

"Fines?" Mac asked with surprise.

"You don't even want to know!" Connie retrieved the heavy book and set it back on the dresser.

Both women tilted their heads, admiring the dress as if it were some sort of sacred oracle.

"The important thing is to keep it preserved," Elizabeth said.

Connie looked at Mac. "For the next generation."

He swallowed hard, wondering if he'd want his own daughter accepting such an enormous responsibility. There might be two Books of Rules by then. But instead of saying so, he just smiled tightly and said, "Right."

"Right! Right!" Gilbert echoed.

Elizabeth eyed the happy couple. "So, you two lovebirds. When's the big day?"

Connie flushed. "I already told you, Mom. We're still working on it."

"Well, don't dillydally forever. We can only keep the dress out of storage so long. Rule number twenty—"

"Four," Connie finished for her.

"Precisely. And now that it's here…" She shot Mac a sly wink. "We might as well use it."

"I'm sure Connie and I will take that into consideration, Mrs. Oliver."

"Please, call me Elizabeth."

"Elizabeth."

"I think I'll just pop down the hall and see how the birthday boy is settling in for the night," she told the others. Connie and Mac started to follow her out the door, but she stopped them with a wave of her hand. "Why don't the two of you stay here and discuss timing a bit? Perhaps being in the presence of the dress will inspire you?"

After she'd shut the door, Connie heaved a sigh. "I'm sorry to have put you through that."

"It was no trouble." He strode toward the dress to examine it more closely. It really was quite nice, for that sort of thing, he supposed. Not that Mac was accustomed to seeing too many of them. "It's pretty special to have something like this in your family." He met Connie's gaze. "You're very lucky to get to wear it."

Her eyes flashed with hurt, then watered slightly. "I can't believe you actually said that."

"What? What did I say?"

Connie brought a hand to her chest as she spoke. "That I was so lucky to get to wear it?"

"Well, aren't you?" he asked, dumbfounded.

She huffed. "In a perfect world, yes. In this world—the one that you and I live in? —I don't see it happening any time soon. Do you?"

Mac felt horrible that he'd somehow inadvertently offended her. "Connie, I didn't mean to make you—"

"To what, Mac? Rub in the fact that my family has ordered up the traditional wedding gown, and Constance Marie Oliver is—once again—without a groom?"

"I'm here as long as you need me," he said softly.

"Oh good," she said, her voice coming out in a whimper as tears leaked from her eyes. "That means until the end of the weekend, doesn't it?"

She reached up a hand to wipe back her tears and raced from the room as Mac tried to stop her. "Connie, wait!"

But it was too late. She'd already bolted out and slammed the door. Mac looked down, feeling his boot had caught in something. Oh God, it was the train of the sacred dress. He jumped back with a start, his boot tip yanking the length of fabric forward. "Noooo!" Mac yelped as the mannequin began teetering in the opposite direction. He lunged to catch it, his knees crashing into the front of the dress. *Rip.* Mac's stomach clenched at the sickening tearing sound as he and the mannequin tumbled headlong onto the carpet. The mannequin's head hit the floor and popped off with a *crack*, rolling across the floor like a bowling ball with a swirling bridal veil attached. "Holy crap, I've killed her!" Mac cried with a moan.

"Holy crap! Holy crap!" Gilbert parroted. "Killed her! Killed her! Killed her!"

Great, now I've got a witness. Mac scrambled to his feet and carefully righted the mannequin. But, try as he might, he couldn't get the torn dress to stay up or the severed head to stay on. "Oh boy," he breathed as his heart beat faster. "I'm doomed."

To his horror, the bird began singing to the tune of "Here Comes the Bride."

"Doom-doom-de-doom! Doom-doom-de-doom! Squawk!"

Mac ran his fingers through his hair, trying to gather his thoughts.

"Holy crap! I've killed her! Killed her! Killed her! Killed her!"

Mac looked toward the corner and gritted his teeth.

Ollie stopped Connie as she raced down the hall, sobbing. "Hey, sis, what's the… Have you been crying?"

She met her brother's gaze with bleary eyes. "It's Mac," she said with a sniff. "I just can't do this."

"What's he done?" Ollie asked combatively. "Because if he's hurt you, I swear—"

Connie quickly shook her head. "It's nothing like that."

"Well, then, what is it?"

She heaved a breath. "I don't know if I can go through with it anymore."

"Marrying Mac? But why not? I mean, hey," Ollie said sympathetically, "I know he's a little different, doesn't exactly fit in around here. But he just needs some time around us, and we'll get to know him. If you love him, Connie, then the rest of the family is bound to. I mean, eventually."

"Even Grandpa?" she asked, raising her chin.

"Especially Grandpa. All he wants is for you to be happy. You know that."

"No. What he wants is for me to wear that stupid dress."

"Hey, listen to me. That dress isn't stupid. It's been an Oliver family tradition for years. All right, I'll admit at first I thought the idea was sort of quirky, but now that I've seen how all the other women have gotten into it, I find it kind of…nice."

"Really?"

"Yeah. Really. I mean, if Trudy wanted to wear it, I wouldn't be opposed."

"*Trudy?* You can't mean…?"

"Not getting anywhere close to thinking about it until we've both finished school. But it is on the back burner, if you know what I mean." He grinned, and Connie hugged him soundly.

"That's wonderful, Ollie!"

"Yeah, it's cool. But mum's the word. Okay? I don't want any cats out of the bag for a long while. It's not like I'm asking tomorrow. Besides," he said with a grin. "You're the bride in the spotlight for now."

"I am, aren't I?"

Ollie had a clue what would make her feel better. "I was just headed to the kitchen for some Rocky Road ice cream. Want to join me?"

"After a double dessert and that enormous catered dinner? Are you kidding? You bet!" she said, racing him down the stairs.

Mac shut the door to the gold room behind him and wiped his brow with the back of his sleeve.

"Sneaking a peek at *the dress*?" Linda asked as she and Beau strolled by, linked arm in arm.

Mac felt the blood drain from his face. "No...I... Actually, um..."

"Hey, isn't that supposed to be bad luck before the wedding?" Beau asked.

"That's only when the bride is in it," Mac replied with a croak.

"Yeah," Linda said, playfully poking her husband in the ribs. "Don't be such a stickler for details."

Beau laughed out loud as they snuggled together and continued on their merry way down the hall.

Mac heaved a sigh.

What on earth am I going to do now?

Chapter Seven

Early the next morning in the billiard room,
Wendell Senior dismissed his nurses, then stealthily
rose from his wheelchair, taking his favorite putter in
his hands. How he missed the game, he thought, taking
a broad practice swing. He could see the golf course
behind him through the plate glass window. He and
Melissa had commissioned some men to install it
shortly after they'd bought the vineyard, and for forty-
eight years, Wendell had never missed an afternoon of
golf. He'd played on through rain, wind, and sun, ever
improving his skill. It was just a shame circumstances
and his failing health had forced him into this chair.
Though he did seem to rally some days, he was
concerned things were getting worse. But if his earlier
years of smoking cigars had caused him emphysema, he
didn't want to know it. Best to live out the rest of his
life as well as he could without any further diagnoses
getting in the way. Every time he asked his doctors if he
was dying, they said yes. Then again, they assured him,
so were they. Everybody went one day at a time.
Wendell Senior didn't find this very funny, given his
more limited time. Sure, one might make a joke at fifty.
At eighty now, the joke was on him.

He heard the door creak open and scrambled back
into his chair.

"Father? Are you in here?" It was Junior with
Elizabeth, his bride. The boy had really lucked out with
that one. She was kind and pretty and ever the good
wife. Plus, she had a solid head on her shoulders and
had been a big help in running the business. Wendell

Senior would be able to go to his grave in peace, leaving Wendell Estates Wines in his son's and Elizabeth's capable hands. Now his final task remained in marrying off his granddaughter. But seriously, couldn't she have made a more careful choice for herself?

Wendell pushed back in his chair and set his putter aside. "Yes, I'm here."

"Elizabeth and I were hoping to have a moment to talk with you."

Wendell frowned, feeling a scolding coming on.

"Where are your nurses?" Elizabeth asked, looking around.

"I sent them out for lattes," Wendell answered, feeling grumpy. "I don't need them around twenty-four-seven, you know."

"They look like models, Dad," Junior said. "I'm surprised to hear you complaining."

Wendell waved him away. "It's not the nurses I'm concerned with. It's Connie."

"Precisely what we're here to see you about," Junior said.

"She sent you?"

"No. Elizabeth insisted."

Elizabeth took her husband's hand.

Wendell studied them both: the united front. "I see."

"Wendell," Elizabeth said kindly. "We know that you love Connie just as much as we do."

"We also understand that Mac is a little different from the fiancés she's brought home before."

"He took off his clothes at my party!"

Junior drew a breath. "Well, okay, that was unusual. But Elizabeth has an explanation for that."

"An explanation?" He studied his daughter-in-law. "In the sixties, it was free love, then in the seventies came women's lib. In the eighties, it was disco, then hip hop; now, I don't know. But I can tell you one thing. Disrobing at a party is not the norm in any age!"

Elizabeth raised her brow. "It is at bachelor parties."

Wendell stared at his son. "You didn't tell her about...?"

"No, Dad," Junior said quickly before Wendell could accidently spout that whole thing about the girl popping out of Junior's pre-wedding-night cake. "Our point is this. Connie has made her choice in Mac, and we—Elizabeth and I"—he tightly squeezed her hand— "believe that *all of us* should support her."

"What was I last night if not supportive? I *did* suggest that the new couple have the first dance."

"Yes, and that was very nice," Elizabeth said softly.

"We understand your reservations..." Junior began.

"Do you?" Wendell cut in.

"Of course, we do. He's in a different line of work than we're used to."

"And out of work besides," Wendell added. "Ollie filled me in."

"He has plans to rebuild his store," Elizabeth said.

"With what money?"

The three of them looked at each other.

"There's something that doesn't add up about this man."

"Dad, please."

Elizabeth gazed at him with pleading eyes. "Let's just give him this weekend. All right? A little more time to get to know him and prove to us he's not nearly the bad guy you think he is."

"Harrumph."

"Dad?"

Wendell shifted in his chair, feeling out of sorts again. So Mac had a burned-down business and was planning to rebuild, with no visible means of monetary support, as far as any of them could tell. None of this seemed right to Wendell. In fact, it sounded downright suspicious. As if this hiking-boot-wearing Tarzan was out to take financial advantage of his granddaughter. Naturally he wanted her to get married, but to the *right man*, not some tree-swinging stranger she'd picked up off the Internet.

"Wendell?" Elizabeth pressed when he didn't answer. "Please promise you'll at least try."

Mac arose early after having spent a fitful night trying to imagine what he might do to fix his enormous blunder with the dress. It occurred to him he could ask Ollie to borrow some thread and a sewing needle while pretending he needed it to stitch up Ollie's clothes he had ruined. But then Mac reasoned he shouldn't go anywhere near that sacred gown again, especially carrying a sharp instrument. It probably would require professional repair. Somebody trained in working with delicate materials would have to undo the damage Mac had caused. His palms grew moist at the realization he'd need to offer to pay for it, which would probably take all the money from this gig he was earning to begin with. But could he really charge for his time here when he'd made a fiasco of the whole event? First by causing a scene on the dance floor, next by humiliating

Connie to tears…then finally by single-handedly destroying the Oliver family's crowning glory?

He had to get out of this predicament, but how? He'd already promised Connie he'd see this weekend through. And when she'd left him in tears, he'd become more determined than ever to help her. Not for any cash involved, but because it was the right thing to do. Connie was beautiful and intelligent and kind. He hadn't meant to insult her at all by hinting she'd someday wear that dress, because in his heart he absolutely knew she would. She was a terrific woman who would make a wonderful wife, for just the right man.

Mac understood he faced an uphill battle in convincing her family that man could still be him. Particularly after he broke the news about the dress. Shoot, they might aim to behead him just as surely as he'd whacked that hapless mannequin. Mac buttoned up his shirt, hoping for a peaceful outcome, at least one that didn't involve a lot of weeping and wailing. While Mac didn't take himself for much of a chicken, if they beat him hard enough, he might yelp.

Connie rapped lightly on his door and called from outside. "See you downstairs at breakfast!"

Mac swallowed hard, thinking that even if it was scrambled eggs, he was going to have trouble choking it down past the lies and deception welling inside him. How he wished it were Sunday and he was on his way out of here! Mac laid his hand on the doorknob, then pulled himself up short. Once he was out of here, there'd be no more Connie. Since she was part of this whole sham, once their deal was done, she'd be gone from his life too. But he was okay with that, wasn't he? He barely knew the girl, after all, and she scarcely knew him. She was about to learn a lot more about him very quickly, though. Like what an enormous klutz he was, Mac thought with a gulp.

Mac took his seat at the elegant breakfast table beside Connie. She couldn't help but think he looked extra handsome this morning, all freshened up from his shower. Connie was a bit embarrassed by the display she'd made last night but had plans to discuss it with Mac later. Upon reflection, she'd seen he hadn't meant to be hurtful in suggesting she'd someday wear the wedding dress. He was just stating this as a matter of course, in keeping with the family tradition. Given her age of thirty-two, it wasn't like eventually finding a husband was totally out of the question. Just because she'd let the first three grooms get away, that didn't mean there wouldn't be others in the offing. She'd made herself feel better in convincing herself of that. That extra helping of Rocky Road had just left her feeling bloated. She was still suffering from a food hangover this morning.

Wendell Senior wheeled into the room, and good-mornings were said all around.

"I want to thank you all for a wonderful party last night," Grandpa Oliver said, as their food was served. "It was quite"—he shot Mac a glance and Mac's neck reddened—"memorable, to say the least."

"We all had a great time," Elizabeth said pleasantly.

Wendell Junior smiled at Mac. "We'd like to thank our new guest for joining us, especially."

"Thank you all for including me."

"Well, go on," Elizabeth urged from the head of the table, "You two don't be shy. You can hold hands."

Connie felt her face on fire. "Oh no, Mother, we don't believe in—"

"PDA," Mac filled in.

"What's that?" Grandpa Wendell wondered.

"Public displays of affection," Ollie explained.

"Oh gosh, Connie," Linda taunted, taking Beau's hand and squeezing it in hers. "For heaven's sake, we do it all the time. Nobody cares," she said with a shrug.

All eyes turned to Connie and Mac as Connie nervously pursed her lips and waited.

"Uh, yeah," Mac said, laying his hand on top of hers on the table before patting it lightly.

"Not like that!" Elizabeth said with a jovial laugh. "For goodness sakes, one would think you've never held hands before." Elizabeth sprang from her chair and came around to where Mac and Connie sat. "There," she said, forcing their hands together. "Isn't that better?"

Mac gave her a tight grin. "Much."

Between the coffee and the flapjacks and the soft-boiled eggs that were being passed around, there wasn't much time for Mac to work in true confessions. He noticed Connie wasn't very hungry this morning, sticking to black coffee and a dry piece of toast. He worried she was still upset with him over his foot-in-mouth comment about her wearing that wedding dress, and hoped to clear the air about his intentions. He couldn't really do that before a full crowd of onlookers, though. And they were watching closely, especially Connie's mom, he thought, taking Connie's hand in his once again as Elizabeth shared a pleased smile.

"So after breakfast, I was thinking you might take Mac on a tour of the vineyard," Elizabeth said.

Linda heaped extra flapjacks on her plate. "That's a great idea, Mom."

"It is indeed," Connie's dad agreed.

"Yes. Why don't you show him around a bit," Wendell Senior added. "Let him get the lay of the land."

Connie turned her eyes on his, and Mac was once more caught up in their magic. "Mac? Would you like to?"

This seemed like a good plan. There were lots of things they had to discuss, and having a bit of privacy for a change would prove helpful. "That sounds great."

Connie led Mac through the rows of vines, explaining the different varieties. It was a pleasant day with a light breeze blowing over the hills and strumming its way through the grapes climbing the supports all around them.

"You know a lot about this business," Mac told her. "Ever consider going into it yourself?"

Connie laughed lightly. "About as far into it I go is opening a bottle of wine. Seriously? It's interesting to me, but it's not the way I want to spend my life."

"How do you want to spend your life?"

She looked over the landscape, growing serious a moment, then met his gaze. It occurred to Mac again that her eyes were the color of the sky as it opened up in summertime splendor above them, speckled by just a few billowy clouds. "Like I said in the car, I'm still figuring that out."

"But you enjoy working at the kids' museum?"

"Oh yeah, I love it. It's just not… I don't know. I'm looking for something more. Something I can feel a passion for. Do you know what I'm saying?"

He looked deep in her eyes, and his heart skipped a beat. "I think I do."

"Like maybe the way you feel about your store."

"It's not just a store to me," he told her.

"What do you mean?"

"It's more like…" *Hmm. How can I explain this?* "More like I get to help folks develop excitement about connecting with the great outdoors. So much of people's lives are spent inside. Inside of buildings, inside of cars or subways, just traveling from place to place, within very tight spaces. A lot of constraints, you know?"

"I know all about constraints, believe me."

"Then maybe you'll understand how liberating it can be for someone to escape all that and get back to basics. Climb a mountain, hike a trail… Paddle a canoe down a quiet stream."

"I've never thought about it like that."

"Sometimes it's good to get away from it all, just to hear yourself think."

"What if I don't like what I have to say when I hear myself think?"

"Well, you're in trouble, then," Mac said with a laugh.

She studied him a moment, the sunlight glinting in her hair. "The truth is, I didn't feel calm at all out in nature. I was terrified."

"That's because you didn't know what you were doing. Or, maybe…" He lowered his voice and leaned toward her. "You just needed the right guide."

"Oh yeah?" she asked, looking up.

"Yeah." He was near enough to kiss her again, and, man, didn't he long to, but they had things to clear up first. "Connie," he told her sincerely, "I'm really sorry I hurt your feelings last night. About the dress. I really didn't mean to."

"I know you didn't." She hung her head with a blush. "I was being oversensitive."

"It's a very tough position your family's put you in."

She raised her head, meeting his eyes. "It wasn't really them. I caused the problem myself."

"I don't see how."

Her lips trembled as she appeared to weigh how much she should tell him. "By making myself believe I loved someone when I didn't."

"Your last fiancé?"

"All of them," she answered quietly.

"Then why? Why did you say yes when they asked you?"

She searched his eyes a lingering moment. "Because maybe I thought I'd never find someone to feel that way about." And when Mac looked in her eyes, he could see it was true. Connie Oliver was someone who hadn't believed in love. At least not for herself. And what a shame that was too, when she was so warm and wonderful and felt just like heaven to hold.

"What do you think now?"

She caught her breath as he moved closer. "I'm not sure."

"Let me try to convince you," he said, his mouth hovering over hers.

"Are we still just pretending?"

His voice grew husky as he took her in his arms. "I hope not."

Mac brought his mouth to hers, and Connie feared she'd died and gone to heaven. His beard was soft and silky against her chin, his moustache lightly tickling her lips as he kissed her sweetly at first, and then with a deeper passion. She'd never felt so swept away by a man, and she longed to stay in this moment forever. While kissing him on the dance floor had been grand, it had nothing on now—with just the two of them embracing in the great outdoors. Connie's pulse beat faster as she realized she was starting to hear herself think. And when her heart talked, her head had to listen. This was no longer make-believe for her. She was falling for Mac.

Chapter Eight

The rest of the group lingered over coffee, discussing Mac's pros and cons. "Well, at least he seems to care for her," Elizabeth said. "Even if he's not touchy-feely."

"I would say their kiss last night proved that different," Beau piped in.

Wendell Senior harrumphed. "That was quite a display. Down to his tartan-plaid boxers."

"At least they looked clean," Linda added before Beau elbowed her.

He leaned over and whispered in her ear. "Keep your eyes on your own man."

"Trust me, I do," she said with a wink.

Ollie blew an exasperated breath. "Look, guys, I already told you. He was borrowing my suit. So it ran a bit tight."

"Why are you so interested in defending him?" Wendell asked.

"I just want you to give the guy a fair shake that's all. Connie was so upset she—"

All eyes turned to him. "Connie was upset?" they asked collectively.

"Well, yeah. I mean, no. Listen, the point is, she was just having second thoughts for a moment. But she got over it." Then he added under his breath, "And she'd probably kill me if she knew I told you."

"But why would she have second thoughts?" his dad asked. "I thought Mac was her *chosen*."

"He is," Ollie answered. "But still… You can't blame Connie for getting cold feet, after all those other times."

"Those times the other guys left her, you mean," Wendell added astutely.

"Exactly."

"None of us wants *that* to happen again," Wendell Junior said flatly.

Elizabeth dabbed her mouth with her napkin. "No. We don't."

"No, indeed," Beau echoed. He turned toward Linda, whose eyes were as big as saucers. "You're being awfully quiet."

"I want the same thing that all of you want," she answered with a squeak. "For Connie to be happy."

As the breakfast dishes were cleared, they all decided they should go take a peek at the wedding dress. Nobody there besides Elizabeth had seen it, and Wendell couldn't wait to get a look at his late wife's gown, which brought back so many happy memories. He motioned his nurses along, who steered him into the elevator. "I'll meet the rest of you upstairs," he told the others, disappearing behind metal doors.

Mac held Connie's hand as they walked toward the main house. After an incredibly sexy kissing session in the vineyard, she'd taken him through the production part of the operation, showing him everything from the large oak casks to the automated wine bottler. It must have been something growing up around a thriving business like this one. It occurred to Mac for the first time that, in her own way, Connie had developed just as much appreciation for the land as he had. She just wasn't as comfortable staying out in the open after dark, when there wasn't a celebratory awning strung with festive lights hanging overhead.

During the tour, they'd talked easily, joking with each other like old friends. Not wanting to break the spell between them, he'd put off telling her as long as he could. Now that the moment of truth was near, Mac had to face his fears.

"Connie," he said, stopping her when they stepped onto the back patio. "There's something I need to tell you about the dress."

"Grandma Oliver's wedding dress?" she asked, her eyes questioning. "What about it?"

Mac hated himself for having to say it, mostly because he worried she'd despise him afterward, when everything had been going so well. "I had a little…accident."

Connie halted in her tracks, her face registering horror. "Okay," she said, catching her breath. "First define *little*…then define *accident*."

Elizabeth pressed open the door to the gold room, then yelled in shock, "The dress! It's ruined!"

Ollie's mouth dropped open. "She's been decapitated."

Wendell wheeled into the room with a furor. "Who on earth could have done this?"

"Squawk!" Gilbert said. "Holy crap! I killed her! Killed her! Killed her! Squawk!"

Linda cupped her hand to her mouth. "He didn't."

Beau rolled his eyes toward his wife. "Who didn't?"

"Well, hey there, buddy!" Gilbert replied. "Squawk!"

Elizabeth shut her eyes and counted to ten. "I think I'm getting a migraine."

"This was Mac's doing?" Junior asked in disbelief.

Beau turned toward Linda. "Who else could it have been?"

She blinked.

"Do you know something about this, daughter?" Junior asked sternly.

Linda's face got all pink and puffy, like she was about to burst out crying.

"Linda?" her mother pressed.

"We never thought it would come to this!" she said with a wail.

"What do you mean?" her grandpa asked.

"He's not even her real fiancé!" Linda's voice cracked in despair. "He's a fake!" She spilled the whole sordid story as the others gaped, and Elizabeth rapidly fanned her face with her hands.

Beau peered out the window. "Look! They're on the patio!"

Ollie gritted his teeth and raced from the room. "I'm gonna get that guy!"

"I'm coming too!" Junior said, tearing after him.

Wendell wheeled himself toward the elevator as fast as he could, his nurses trailing. "Get me downstairs—quickly," he commanded.

Beau rushed forward just in time to catch Elizabeth, who fainted from shock.

Ollie stormed onto the patio and socked Mac in the face before he could defend himself.

"Wait! Stop!" Connie yelped. "What are you doing?"

"Do you have any idea what he's done?"

Connie gasped. "But he said it was an accident!"

"An accident?" Ollie rubbed his knuckles while Mac massaged his struck jaw. "Is that what he calls his little game of *pretend*?"

Her knees felt weak. "What?"

"The jig is up," her dad said. "This man is a liar and a cheat, and he's destroyed the one thing this family holds dear."

"The dress?" Connie asked in stunned disbelief. "Is it really ruined?"

"It's not just the dress he's destroyed," Grandpa Oliver said, wheeling onto the patio. "It's this family. He's broken our trust."

Mac began his apology, his face red from the neck up. "Sir, I'm so sorry. I'll offer to pay, anyth—"

"Can it," Junior said flatly. "We'll thank you to pack your bags and get out of here. You can call a cab from your room."

Mac looked around the patio at all of them. Even Linda and Beau were there, with Elizabeth leaning weakly against Beau's arm. "But if you'd just let me explain—"

Wendell Senior stared at him, indignant. "What? That you agreed to accept twenty thousand dollars in cash for your participation in this little ploy?" He wheeled toward Mac with a scowl. "Let me tell you something, mister. My granddaughter might make mistakes, but she deserves better than that."

"Connie?" Mac asked, his face etched with pain. "Is that what you want? For me to go?"

She couldn't see how his staying would make things any better. This whole thing had exploded like an enormous atom bomb, and now pieces of shrapnel were everywhere. She wanted to find her voice but felt muted by the hurt welling within her. She couldn't get a damn thing right. Not even in make-believe with Mac. How could she have been foolish enough to dream things would work out, when everything had started with such a big lie?

She dropped her face in her hands and wept with humiliation as he turned and walked away. "You didn't have to be so hard on him," she said. "I had a part in this as well."

"Yes," her mom said, "a very big part, it seems. We'll need to talk that over."

"Not now. Please, not now," Connie said, her heart breaking. For the first time in her life, she'd thought she'd begun to feel something authentic for a man, but now she guessed that had been a lie too.

Chapter Nine

Six weeks later, Hank sunned himself on a rock while Mac stared stoically ahead.

"I really appreciate you inviting me on this little excursion. It's been just like camping with a corpse."

"You don't know what it's been like, losing her." He appeared wistful a moment. "It's just like Chance."

Hank lifted his head to look at him. "You mean like fate?"

"No, my yellow lab. I lost him in the woods when I was nine and never saw him again."

"Man, that's heartbreaking. In fact, that's got to be the saddest thing I've ever heard."

Mac stared at him poignantly.

"Up until now. This thing with Connie. It's much worse."

Mac sighed, surveying the forest.

Hank sat up, resting his forearms on his knees. "Have you tried calling?"

"Dozens of times."

"What does she say?"

"That some things can't be undone, that's what."

"Well, maybe she's right." Mac turned toward him. "You did cause quite a nasty scene with her family. Maybe you should have shot that bird."

"Thanks, Hank."

"I mean it. If that little snitch hadn't squawked—"

"The whole thing would have unraveled anyway."

Hank hated seeing his friend like this, all down and defeated. "How long do you suppose it'll be before you snap out of it?"

"Forever. Why?"

"Because…" he said, drawing out the word. "Candy and I are going to a movie this weekend—"

"Candy? You're dating a woman named Candy? Get real." He shot Hank a grin. "What is she? Sweet on you?"

"Great! You're feeling better. Being Mr. Smarty-pants."

Mac shook his head.

"So you'll join us, then?"

"Who?"

"Me and Candy… And her friend—"

"No."

"Come on, man."

"No way."

"Just one date."

"Not interested."

"You're going to die a bachelor if it kills you."

"I have wonderful news from New York!" Elizabeth proclaimed as she sat at Connie's kitchen table. "The dress is going to live."

Connie breathed a sigh of relief, hugging her mother. "Thank goodness the damage wasn't permanent."

"The word is no one will ever know…unless they use a magnifying glass."

"You didn't tell Aunt Mona?"

"Heavens! And encourage her to add another chapter in that dreadful book? Not on your life."

Connie walked to the counter and poured them two cups of coffee. "I'm glad it's all worked out." She shot her mom a sad glance. "Most of it anyhow."

"Has he called?" Elizabeth asked with a worried frown.

"A couple of times."

"And?"

"And it was hard. Awkward. There really isn't much to say."

"How about let's get together for dinner?"

Connie sat with surprise. "That's a little forward."

Elizabeth leaned over, lightly touching her arm. "Come on, you're miserable without him."

"But I thought none of you could stand Mac?"

Elizabeth sipped from her cup, then set it down. "It wasn't Mac, per se, but rather the shock of everything surrounding him at the time."

"Like the tattered dress?"

"That didn't help."

"People make mistakes."

"Of course they do." Elizabeth studied her daughter. "How do you know you're not making one now?"

Connie thoughtfully gazed at her mom. "Sometimes things are too weird to go back, you know? It's not like we were ever really dating."

"I'm sorry, Connie," her mom said, sounding as if she meant it. After a beat, she said, "Tell me about that new venture of yours. Sugar Shots, you say it's called?"

Connie felt her face brighten. "Yes, and I've got a couple of investors already. Parents from the children's museum."

"That's wonderful. What will you sell?"

"Baked goods and photographs of what I make."

"I'm not sure I understand."

"Sugar Shots will be a bakery boutique," Connie explained, "focusing on miniatures. Miniature pies, miniature cakes, little tiny cookies, and the like."

"Oh, how cute!"

"Yes. And I plan to photograph everything."

"What do you mean?"

"Well, when I cater a party with a selection of minis styled to the hostess's direction, I'll take commemorative photos of the food's presentation and frame them like this." She produced an example of a high-resolution photograph in a frame overlaid with the words, *Happy fifth birthday, Minnie.* The picture was of a layered "cake" made from five tiers of tiny pink cupcakes crowned with confectionary tiaras.

"That's darling," Elizabeth said. "Very clever."

"The cool thing is, I'll keep duplicate photos in the shop and hang them on the walls. That way, I'll have samples for other customers to examine as I'm building my client base."

Her mom's face glowed warmly. "I'm so proud of you for thinking this out."

"I knew I'd get around to something eventually. My mind had just been too cluttered to see the whole thing through."

"What helped clear it?"

"A bit of fresh air."

"Huh?"

"Have you ever noticed that when you're outdoors—like biking or something?–you can think that much better?"

"No, I can't say that I have." She shrugged and smiled brightly. "The important thing is, it's worked for you. I'm so happy for you, Connie. After all this time, you're finally on your way."

Six months later, Mac stood with satisfaction outside his new storefront. He'd worked hard to obtain the bank loan, but the interest rate he'd secured was a good one, and he had no doubt he'd be turning a profit shortly. He heard a happy bark and spun in surprise to see Hank ambling up from the parking lot. Well, what do you know? Carting a little Labrador puppy, with a bright red ribbon tied around its neck.

"What's this?" he asked as Hank approached.

"A little house-warming gift."

Mac was immediately taken in by the huge puppy paws and big brown eyes. He accepted the dog, scratching it under the chin. "Hey there, little guy. What's your name?"

"Chance," Hank said with a grin. "The Second."

The pup wiggled up to lick Mac's face, and a lump welled in his throat.

"Thanks, man…" He slapped Hank's arm, steeling his emotions. "You're the best."

Hank's gaze swept across the store's façade. "Looking good. When do you open up?"

"First of next week."

"That's awesome. Congrats."

The dog gave Mac another puppy kiss, and he laughed heartily, snuggling it close. "You really were crazy nice to do this."

Hank surveyed his friend. "Got plans for the rest of the afternoon?"

"Me and Chance?" Mac asked with a laugh. "Not really."

"Then let's drive into town. Grab a cup of coffee."

"Hank," Mac said with a grin. "You've got a date."

Hank chuckled, patting the puppy's head. "It's about time."

As they approached the café district, Hank said, "There are a lot of new places that have opened up around here. Just let me know when you want to stop."

Mac held the puppy in his lap, seeing Hank was right. There were a number of shops he didn't recognize, including one with its front window filled with photographs of… Wait a minute. Food? Something vague tugged at the back of his mind, but he wasn't sure what.

"Sugar Shots?" he said to Hank. "Have you heard of that one?"

"Is it a coffee shop?"

Mac didn't know, but for some reason, the name intrigued him. "How about we check it out?"

"Sounds good to me," Hank said, pulling into the next vacant parking space.

When Mac and Hank entered the store, they saw it was a cute bakery. They did sell coffee and lattes and cappuccinos…and chai, along with a whole host of miniature confections, ranging from cupcakes to little iced scones. It was a small operation, with a smattering of tables for two near the big front window. Only a few of them were occupied by well-coiffed ladies swapping gossip over java and tiny jelly donuts. No one was behind the counter at the moment. But one of the ladies assured them the owner would be right out, as she oohed and aahed over Mac's puppy. "We'll have to ask about the dog," Hank said.

Mac noted two empty tables on the sidewalk beside the shop's door. "It's all right. We can sit outside." He cradled the puppy in his arms and scanned the framed pictures on the walls. That was when it hit him. The name of the woman who loved taking photos of food...

"Connie!" he cried with surprise as she bustled out of the kitchen with a teapot and a basket of goodies on a tray. She was moving fast, on a straight trajectory toward him and the dog.

Blue eyes lit up with wonder. "Mac?"

Chance squirmed in Mac's arms. "Whoa there, fella," he said, trying to control the wiggling dog. He lowered the pup to the floor, and Chance bounded toward Connie, barking excitedly. She glanced down, hefting her heavy tray higher. "Well, hello... Whoa... Whoa!" she yelped. To her horror, the tray tilted and its contents began to slide. The pup yapped happily underneath the tilting tray, on the verge of having the whole weight of it dropped on him as it slid from Connie's grip. "Oh no!" she cried, watching the scalding hot teapot and everything else plummet.

Mac leaped forward, pouncing on Connie and pushing the tray to the side while calling out like a madman, "Chance!" Both lost their footing and tumbled, but Mac held her close, breaking her fall with his arms behind her and her head cradled in his hands.

The dog darted under a table with a whimper as the teapot exploded in streams of hot liquid and ceramic shards, and scones bounced out of their basket.

Connie looked up at Mac, who lay flat on top of her, pinning her to the floor. "Are you all right?" he asked, his face coloring beneath his beard.

"I think so," she said, still reeling from the moment. Of all people! Mac McCormack, that incredibly handsome outdoorsman. And right here on top of her. Connie realized café patrons were staring and felt her temperature rise.

He seemed lost in her eyes, then snapped himself out of it. "Good. That's really good," he said, rolling off her so she could once again breathe. He offered her his hands and pulled her into a sitting position. Chance scrambled out from under a table and loped over, picking up a scone along the way.

"Why, who's this?" Connie asked with delight, as the pup dropped the scone and scrambled up in her lap, putting its paws on her shoulders to lick her face.

Mac rocked back on his knees with a smile. "Chance."

Connie laughed at the pup's tickling wet kisses. "Chance?" she asked, patting his furry head.

"The Second!" Hank called from nearby.

Connie glanced at him and smiled. She hadn't even noticed he was here. Of course, that would have been difficult with a gorgeous blast from her past landing on top of her. It was hard to forget what being in Mac's arms had been like. Harder still to erase the memory of his sexy kisses. She'd tried to forget and move on with her life, and she'd really been doing quite well. In her mind, she'd totally convinced herself that she was over him. Now, seeing him in person, her heart felt otherwise. By the look in his eyes, he felt otherwise too. She didn't know if he'd planned it or if serendipity had brought him to her shop. But one way or another, it seemed a magical twist of fate. A sign too blatant to ignore. She grinned at Mac and tilted her chin, hoping that he'd say yes. "Second chance?"

His face warmed all over as he held her gaze. "I'd like that."

Epilogue

A small flower girl tossed white rose petals down the aisle ahead of her as she strode in perfectly measured steps. Connie stood behind her in the narthex, glowing radiantly. Mac could spot her from the front of the church and couldn't wait for her to join him at the altar so the priest could make her his bride. Of all the crazy things that had happened to him in his life, falling out of that tree and nearly landing on Connie had been the single most important. For that hapless event had set in motion a whole series of others that led to this wonderful moment here.

Grandpa Oliver wheeled up beside Connie, prepared to escort her down the aisle. She'd talked it over with her parents and all agreed it would be the highlight of her grandfather's life. He had lived to see his final granddaughter married in the family dress, and, my, didn't she look beautiful wearing it. Just like an angel, in fact. Mac chuckled to himself, recalling his initial impression of Connie with a halo, and knew that, for the eternity of their marriage, he would always be in heaven.

At the back of the church, Connie caught sight of Mac standing beside Hank at the altar. He was a vision in a tuxedo and boutonniere, and had offered to shave his beard, but Connie had said, *"Don't you dare."* She adored her rugged mountain man exactly as he was and looked forward to many years of proving just how much she loved him. It was June fifteenth, and they'd set this date on purpose. It was precisely one year since they'd met during Connie and Linda's ill-fated girls' getaway. Connie smiled to herself, thinking that sometimes mishaps led to happy endings, and that when you found the right guy, free falling wasn't so hard.

"You look beautiful," Grandpa Oliver told her. "Just like your grandmother."

"I'll take that as a very big compliment."

Her grandpa glanced sideways as her brother approached. To Connie's surprise, he was carrying a cane. He passed it to her grandpa, who accepted it with a nod. "Thanks, Ollie."

Connie looked from one to the other in wonder. "What's this?"

"I've dreamed of this day your whole life," her grandpa said. "And I promised your grandmother long ago I'd see it through."

To her amazement, he steadied his cane on the floor and leaned forward. A few hoarse coughs erupted from his chest, but he pounded it with his fist, quieting himself.

"Grandpa, maybe—"

"Please." He met her eyes as he stood on shaky legs. "Indulge me." He stabilized himself, then straightened, shooting her a grin. "I've been practicing up."

Tears welled in Connie's eyes as she took her grandfather's arm. "I love you so much."

"I know you do," he said with a smile. "And I love you. The beautiful thing is"—he glanced down the aisle toward Mac—"now he will love you too."

The processional began to play, and Connie's heart soared. This was the best day of her life, and they were all about to get even better. As her grandpa led her forward, guests turned in amazement with gasps and whispers behind raised hands. Yes, he'd surprised them all and rallied to this special occasion. Connie would never forget this day or her grandfather. He would live in her heart forever, and the family tradition would carry on.

The End

A Note from the Author

Thanks for reading *Must-Have Husband*, a story that is based on a true tradition within my own family. Many years ago, my grandmother envisioned an heirloom wedding gown for her descendants. I was bride number fifteen to wear it, and to date twenty-nine brides have donned the family dress. If you enjoyed this book, please help other people find it.

1. This book is lendable, so loan it to a friend who you think might like it so that she (or he) can discover me, too.

2. Help other people find this book: write a review.

3. Sign up for my newsletter so that that you can learn about the next book as soon as it's available. Write to GinnyBairdRomance@gmail.com with "newsletter" in the subject heading.

4. Come like my Facebook page: http://www.facebook.com/GinnyBairdRomance.

5. Comment on my blog: The Story Behind the Story at http://www.goodreads.com.

6. Visit my website: http://www.ginnybairdromance.com for details on other books available at multiple outlets now.

www.ingramcontent.com/pod-product-compliance
Lightning Source LLC
Chambersburg PA
CBHW030643130626
46552CB00002B/999